OPERATION LENINGRAD

Recent Titles by Leo Kessler from Severn House

Writing as Leo Kessler

S.S.Wotan Series
Assault On Baghdad
Death's Eagles
The Great Escape
Hitler Youth Attacks!
Kill Patton
Operation Glenn Miller
Operation Iraq
Patton's Wall
The Screaming Eagles
Sirens of Dunkirk
Wotan Missions

Battle for Hitler's Eagles' Nest
The Blackout Murders
The Churchill Papers
Murder at Colditz
The Blackout Murders

Writing as Duncan Harding

Assault on St Nazaire
Attack New York!
Clash in the Baltic
The Finland Mission
Hell on the Rhine
The Normandie Mission
Operation Judgement
Sink the Ark Royal
Sink the Bismarck
Sink the Cossack
Sink the Graf Spee
Sink HMS Kelly
Sink the Hood
Sink the Prince of Wales
Sink the Scharnhorst
Sink the Tirpitz
Sink the Warspite
Slaughter in Singapore
The Tobruk Rescue

OPERATION LENINGRAD

Leo Kessler

This first world edition published in Great Britain 2005 by
SEVERN HOUSE PUBLISHERS LTD of
9–15 High Street, Sutton, Surrey SM1 1DF.
This first world edition published in the USA 2005 by
SEVERN HOUSE PUBLISHERS INC of
595 Madison Avenue, New York, N.Y. 10022.

British Library Cataloguing in Publication Data

Kessler, Leo, 1926-
Operation Leningrad
1. Saint Petersburg (Russia) - History - Siege, 1941-1944 - Fiction
2. War stories
I. Title
823.9'14 [F]

ISBN 0-7278-6236-7

Except where actual historical events and characters are being described for the storyline of this novel, all situations in this publication are fictitious and any resemblance to living persons is purely coincidental.

Typeset by Palimpsest Book Production Ltd.,
Polmont, Stirlingshire, Scotland.
Printed and bound in Great Britain by
MPG Books Ltd., Bodmin, Cornwall.

Foreword

Operation Leningrad is the latest in a series of novels based on the memoirs of one of the most famous (or infamous, if you like) of the former SS officers, Kuno von Dodenburg, the one-time commander of 'Hitler's Fire Brigade', SS Assault Regiment Wotan. The manuscripts and memoirs of von Dodenburg, written mostly in the spiky hand of Obersturmbannführer von Dodenburg himself on yellowing, poor-quality wartime paper, were discovered in the second-hand section of a well-known Berne *Buchhandlung*. How these papers got to the Swiss bookshop in the Herrengasse is anyone's guess. No one ever found out. Leo Kessler, author of the 'Wotan series', as it has been called over the years, tried very hard to discover the truth and failed. But from the facts contained in these yellowing papers, some of them stamped with the old formula in bright red '*Geheime Reichssache*' (Secret State Paper), Kessler was able to piece together the following account of that bold, arrogant young man with his black cap set at a rakish angle and bearing the dreaded skull-and-crossbones of the Armed SS, who helped to blaze a trail of fear across Europe . . .

In 1935 or thereabouts, Kuno von Dodenburg joined the Berlin *Reitersturm*, a voluntary SS cavalry unit, while he was still in his final year at high school. The von Dodenburgs apparently had always been cavalry officers and his father, the 'General', as he was called, had not objected to Kuno's 'temporary aberration', as he called it; he'd get over it. Privately he told his old cronies of the 'Imperial German Army' that he didn't mind the boy joining the 'black pack' of the SS – for a while. In the *Reitersturm* he'd learn to ride and the voluntary unit was patronized by the cream of Berlin society, including two Hohenzollern princes from the old monarchy, which he had served so loyally, as had his forefathers before him.

But Kuno, now tall, lean and blond, handsome in a harsh, arrogant way, didn't get over it. One year later when he had passed his *Abitur* and it was time to join his father's old regiment, the Fourth Cavalry, Kuno was no longer interested in the *Wehrmacht*. He wanted to be a member of the 'New Order', which, as he put it in the first flush of youthful enthusiasm, 'would cleanse Europe of its decadence'. Now young men would give the orders.

He volunteered and was accepted for the Waffen SS's most elite formation, '*die Leibstandarte Adolf Hitler*', Hitler's personal bodyguard regiment. Unlike his contemporaries from the old traditional military families, he didn't become an officer-cadet immediately. Instead he served in the ranks as a simple soldier for several months (this would come in useful when in his papers he had to describe the life of the ordinary SS trooper; something that writer Leo Kessler used to full advantage). Finally von Dodenburg was accepted for officer training and was sent to the SS Cadet School at Bad Tölz in Bavaria, one day to be the headquarters of no less a person than 'Old Blood an' Guts' General George Patton.

One year on von Dodenburg graduated with honours and was posted to the staff of Reichsführer SS Heinrich Himmler (probably Himmler, a snob, liked to have aristocratic young officers around him; they lent class to the 'upstart SS').

It is clear, though he never mentioned the fact in his papers, that in that first year as Himmler's junior adjutant, von Dodenburg learned something of the truth behind the facade of the 'New Order'. Indeed there is a photograph extant of a very youthful Kuno von Dodenburg standing just behind Himmler as they inspected shaven-headed prisoners at Dachau Concentration Camp outside Munich. If he knew about the camps, he must have known, too, the cruel manner in which the National Socialist State treated its political opponents and, naturally, Germany's Jews.

But in that last year before the outbreak of war, young Kuno came predominantly under the influence of a senior member of Hitler's staff, the so-called 'Duke of Swabia'. He was SS Brigadeführer Gottlob Berger, an unscrupulous, energetic World War One veteran. Berger was Himmler's principal confidant. In his customary modest manner, he wrote of his chief many years later: 'The Reichsführer confides in me and tells me things personally which he would never do unless he was completely at ease with me.'

Berger, as flashy and self-opinionated as he was, was, however, Kuno von Dodenburg's military mentor. He inspired the young officer with his own concept of a new type of fighting soldier: a hunter-poacher-athlete, an ideological warrior who was prepared to die for his Führer and the cause of National Socialism.

In Berger's opinion, which carried a lot of weight in the Armed SS, the traditional *Wehrmacht* generals wanted to fight any future war as they had done World War One: with a citizen army based on mass conscription. Berger, on the other hand, believed in a highly trained and fast-moving small military elite, as exemplified by the SS. It is clear now that von Dodenburg was fired by the 'Duke of Swabia's' concept of modern warfare and when Germany marched on Poland in the autumn of 1939 he requested an immediate transfer back to his old unit, *die Leibstandarte*, hoping to be able to put Berger's theories into practice.

He and other enthusiastic young officers like him, Jochen Peiper, Gerd Bremer etc. etc. were able to do so, but at a tremendous cost in human life. In von Dodenburg's first battle at Bzura (Central Poland) he was wounded and awarded the Iron Cross, Second Class. It was to be the first of his six wounds and the first, too, of his many decorations which ended just before the fall of Berlin in 1945 with the Knight's Cross, complete with Swords and Diamonds.

The years passed. Von Dodenburg and his unit were always at the front as the 'Führer's Fire Brigade'. Holland, France, Jugoslavia, Greece, country after country, victory after victory: nothing seemed able to stop the might and fury of German arms. But it was in Russia that von Dodenburg started to show his real talent as a commander of genius. In the winter when the steam began to go out of Germany's 'Operation Barbarossa' and the supposedly beaten Red Army launched a surprise attack over the River Donetz, the newly promoted Captain von Dodenburg was ordered by his battalion commander, Colonel Geier – 'the Vulture', of whom we shall hear more in due course – to break through to the trapped 240th Infantry Division. This German division with hardly any transport was trying to escape the trap in that terrible Russian winter although encumbered with over fifteen hundred wounded.

Von Dodenburg didn't hesitate. Cutting through a whole Siberian rifle corps with his tanks and panzer grenadiers, Wotan with von Dodenburg broke through. Forming an armoured defensive position around the infantry, which were moving at a snail's pace, with its long convoy of ambulances and horse-drawn carts laden with their cargoes of human misery, von Dodenburg battled his way back to the River Donzte, his start-line.

There he discovered to his chagrin that the ice-covered Soviet river was incapable of supporting his heavy Mark IV tanks. Another commander might have destroyed his armour and crossed the river on foot over the pontoon bridges now being used by the survivors of the battered German infantry division. Not von Dodenburg. Wotan battled its way along another twenty kilometres of the river line, fighting off massive Soviet attacks. Finally he found an intact bridge which would bear his precious tanks. No one was surprised when the Führer personally presented Kuno von Dodenburg with his Knight's Cross and the handsome cropped-blond SS officer started to receive fan mail from admiring females, many of whom wrote openly they wanted his child, as if he were a movie star like Johannes Hesters or Luis Trenker.

But the ordinary rank-and-file of Wotan knew that von Dodenburg was not simply a glory hunter like so many of these dashing young officers of the Armed SS were. He was not afraid to grab a rifle and fight side-by-side with his 'stubble-hoppers', as his panzer grenadiers called themselves cynically. Indeed on one occasion when the regiment was attacked by the feared new T-34 Soviet tanks, he went 'tank-busting' with an infantryman's bazooka while the rest of the troops went to ground hurriedly. Within the hour he had knocked out four of the monsters and had completely reversed the position. Then when his shame-faced men emerged from their holes, he didn't chide them. Instead he said simply, handing back the 'stove-pipe', as the bazooka was called, 'I suppose that qualifies me for the combat infantryman's badge, comrades, eh?' Thereafter his men loved him and, as one of them who has featured greatly in the Kessler series, Sergeant Schulze, maintained right to the bitter end, 'We'd have followed the CO to hell and back – and then some.'

But Russia left its scars on von Dodenburg, as Leo Kessler makes clear in his current work. They were both physical and emotional. Again he was wounded. But he had become accustomed to having his flesh scourged by the enemy, French, British, American, Russian etc. etc., at period intervals. By 1942 it had become more than the annual blood-letting, however. He had gone to Russia, confident of victory and the holy cause of National Socialism. But when he came out of the devastating defeat of German arms on the Leningrad Front in 1942, his shattered arms hanging by a few shreds of bloody flesh and sinews, his confidence had been badly hurt. In the old cavalry hospital in the university town of Heidelberg where – again the Patton connection – 'Old Blood an' Guts' died three years later, he started to take a look at himself and his country during the long period of his recovery.

Unfortunately, just before the generals' plot to kill Hitler in July 1944, General von Dodenburg, Kuno's father, thought it was wiser to destroy Kuno's papers dealing with his thoughts on the Führer and the whole Nazi regime. But from the odd scrap of paper and letters which the aged general overlooked, it was clear that his son had become a member of the German resistance to the National Socialist State, at least in spirit. One fragment that Kuno penned in his spiky handwriting while in Heidelberg reads: 'German occupation in the East is a masterpiece of ineptitude. Within a year since 1941, it has achieved the astonishing feat of turning the pro-German slavic peoples there who had originally welcomed us as liberators from the Soviet yoke in June that year into fiercely anti-German partisans, roaming the great forests of the area, thirsting for our blood.' Another records that 'German policy is one of ruthless brutality, employing methods used centuries ago against ignorant black slaves in Africa, executed by uneducated louts in uniform who proclaim themselves members of the "Master Race".' By one year later a despondent Kuno was even attacking his own formation of which he had once been so proud. In a letter to Obersturmbannführer Jochen Peiper, commanding the panzer regiment of Kuno's old regiment '*Die Leibandare*' and now the SS's leading light, he wrote: 'I'm always hearing about the spirit of the SS. It's a lot of bullshit, Jochen, believe you me. It doesn't exist any more.'

Still Kuno was a patriotic officer of the old school, despite his training at the hands of the 'Duke of Swabia'. He couldn't just walk away from the front and become a 'rear-echelon swine', sitting at some desk in Berlin, waiting for the end of the war and the destruction of Hitler's vaunted '1,000-year Reich'. He went back to Wotan. He became the youngest colonel in the Armed SS, leading his young volunteers with such reckless bravery, it was as if he could not wait for an enemy bullet to put an end to a life he now, obviously, regarded as wasted. But he was not fated to die on the battlefield. In the last great offensive of the German Army in the West, the 'Battle of the Bulge', he was captured when his Tiger tank was knocked out by a lone US bazooka man, Al Rosenfeld, from New York's Queens, who two weeks before had been a cook in a rear-line unit in Belgium.

Von Dodenburg spent two years thereafter in American POW camps, 'trying find myself,' as he explained to fellow SS officers, who wondered at his strange apathy. In the summer of '47, reformed or not, he 'found' himself and escaped from the Dachau POW compound, where the miserable wretches of the concentration camp had been replaced by SS war criminals. With the help of the 'ODESSA', the secret SS escape organization, he escaped across the Bavarian Alps into Italy. Here, under an alias and supported by SS funds spirited into supposed 'neutral' Switzerland during the war, he started to write. He turned his wartime experiences with Wotan into poorly written, thinly disguised fiction. But the books with their gaudy covers didn't sell – the SS had become a dirty word, especially in Kuno's native country Germany.

In the late forties, the SS money started to dry up. In the new Federal Republic of the 'economic miracle', no one wanted to risk his new-found wealth and position by being associated with the SS. Kuno von Dodenburg struggled to make ends meet. Now he worked as a third-class cheap translator of German and Italian in a fourth-rate Italian agency, sometimes living off cheap red wine and bread and olives. At night, however, he still worked feverishly on his accounts of long dead young men who had once fought and died in the ranks of SS Assault Regiment Wotan. Why, he never knew. Perhaps he felt it was important to give them – and himself – some kind of memorial.

His health started to give out. In '51 he was befriended by a plain motherly woman who worked at the Italian agency. The Italian typist became his mistress – a bit of a come-down for a man who had once bedded the cream of the German aristocracy and beautiful women all over Europe. But she was kind and he moved in with her. Under her doting care, his fragile health improved, but only for a while.

In 1952 Kuno von Dodenburg was rushed to Rome's German Hospital, a dying man. The Jewish bazooka man of December '44, who was now back in Queens as a short-order cook in a deli, had done a better job than he had thought. He had always maintained that he should have been given at least the Bronze Star for having 'knocked out the Nazi bastard!' On the night of 15th June 1952, the day the Allies had captured Rome eight years before, Kuno von Dodenburg, the 'Black Guards'' youngest colonel and most decorated soldier, passed away, attended only by his plump, plain, weeping mistress. It was only with difficulty that she made out his last words, whispered in hoarse hesitant German. 'We were intoxicated by a vision of great power,' he croaked, as she leaned forward to hear, while nuns flitted back and forth like silent white swans. 'It gripped us in a huge frenzy . . . a frenzy of power.' Suddenly, startlingly, he raised himself and bellowed in a voice that had once carried far over parade grounds all over occupied Europe, his right arm outstretched in that old salute, '*Es Lebe Das Sturmregiment Wotan*!'* An instant later he fell back dead . . .

For twenty years or so the von Dodenburg papers and attempts at novels disappeared. In June 1973 they were translated and rewritten by Leo Kessler. The records also formed the basis of his own semi-fictional novels, featuring von Dodenburg and the 'old hares' (*alte Hasen*) of SS Wotan. Through this combination of truth and semi-fiction, the reader of today is able to hear the true voice of the Armed SS, who one might say was transformed by the war from a 'Saul' to a 'Paul'.

Von Dodenburg, once the fanatical supporter of the National Socialist 'New Order' was transformed by the war. Once, in the beginning, he had been proud to belong to that elite formation which became the scourge of Europe. But over the years he started to realize that his comrades were a ruthless, even heartless collection of elite soldiers, who were fighting for an idea which had long lost its validity and for a glory that had vanished years before.

In *Operation Leningrad*, we can see the start of that transformation. In Leo Kessler's account of the amazing *nine-hundred day* siege of the Russian port of Leningrad by the German Army, we are able to trace the young officer's growing disillusionment with a Nazi regime that he had served till then with '*Herz und Seele*' (heart and soul), as the Germans say. It is not a pleasant tale, this loss of faith. But in those days there were no pleasant tales.

Charles Whiting

* Long Live SS Assault Regiment Wotan. *Transl.*

He was a different man. Something had come to him, which had not yet come to us. It was the trial of battle and no one who passes through it is ever quite the same again.

H. Allen

BOOK ONE

The Mission is Proposed

One

'*Greenbeaks*!' One Ball shouted as the strains of the Berlin Garrison Band grew ever louder, heralding Wotan's new recruits, straight from the training depot. Lazily the veterans, 'the old hares', made their way to the windows of their barracks and messes to survey the second lot of cannonfodder SS Assault Regiment Wotan had received since the new war with Russia.

'The Bull', the regiment's gigantic and brutally muscled sergeant-major, thrust out his massive chest, so that it appeared he might burst his tunic at any moment, his broad face brick-red and brutal under his too small steel helmet. He swung round – his body worked as if on rusty springs – and faced the handful of 'old hares', the light patches on their faded and darned uniforms indicating that they had once been NCOs who had been demoted for some military crime or other. 'All right, you bunch o' piss-pansies. I want these greenbeaks to be treated right. No snide remarks or cheeky comments. I'll carve the balls off'n any man who does – with *a blunt razor*!' The Bull glared at them to make sure they understood his awful threat. It left the old hares cold. After Russia nothing could frighten them any more.

Now the first of the recruits came marching round the corner into barracks following the red-faced, plump, middle-aged bandsmen. For the most part they were blond and well-built and, watching from the regimental office, Kuno von Dodenburg, commander of Wotan's 1st Company, remarked to Major Dietz, the temporary Wotan regiment commander, 'Not a bad bunch, Major. Fit and healthy at least, if nothing else.'

Dietz, still pale from his wound, twisted his new wooden arm around so that he was ready to take the parade when the Bull was ready with the recruits. 'Seen worse, Kuno,' he said without too much conviction. 'But they look so damned green. Straight from their mother's titty, most of them. How they'll survive in Popovland' – he meant Russia – 'only God knows.' He shook his head, obviously a worried man.

'They'll be all right on the day, Major,' Kuno von Dodenburg reassured the acting regiment commander. 'After all they – and we – are the Führer's fire brigade, the elite of the SS. We get only the best of the new recruits.'

'Famous last words, Kuno.'

Watching the new arrivals wheel and begin to form up, while behind them the *Hiwis*[*] followed, pushing handcarts laden with the recruits' heavy gear, with the Bull bellowing angrily, 'Get them frigging Popovs off my parade ground – *at once*!', the old hares cheered and made ribald remarks at the new arrivals' expense.

'Bed-wetters!' they cried and jeered. 'Real piss-pansies!'

'Wankers!' Sergeant Schulze sneered and made an explicit gesture with a right hand that looked like a small steam shovel. 'Five against one. Hair on their frigging palms, the lot of 'em!'

'Virgins – all,' his running mate, Corporal Matz yelled, not to be outdone.

'Show 'em a nice juicy beaver, filled with sack rats,' – he meant 'crabs' – 'and they'd faint clean away. I swear.'

Out of breath with the effort of so much shouting, Schulze shook his head and concluded, 'Bunch of arses-with-ears. Sugar titty and mother's milk. That's what they've bin raised on. Frigging hopeless.' He shook his big head once again as if he couldn't understand the world any longer.

On the parade ground, the Bull signalled the band's drum major, a drinking crony of his. The latter brought his mace down sharply. The band stopped playing immediately. The Bull shouted, 'Parade – stand at ease . . . Stand easily.'

[*] *Hilfsfreiwilligen*, voluntary auxiliaries, former members of the Red Army captured and forced to serve in the *Wehrmacht*. *Transl.*

Gratefully the young recruits shot out their right feet and relaxed. One started to fart, until the Bull's red-eyed gaze fell upon him. He stopped immediately and One Ball sneered, 'Here we go, comrades . . . You have the great honour today of becoming members of the elite of the elite.'

He mimicked the Bull's bellow and Matz said, 'Knock it off, comrade. If the Bull hears yer, he'll have yer behind Swedish curtains' – he meant prison bars – 'in zero comma seconds.'

Schulze raised a middle finger like a hairy pork sausage. 'Let the bugger sit on that,' was his sole comment. For he, too, had heard the big sergeant-major's speech all too often in these last months. Soon the big bastard'd be trying it on with the frightened recruits, getting them to buy him free suds in the taverns all around the barracks, 'bonding us together, old soldier and new recruit,' as he always put it, the greedy swine. Schulze smiled. But let him get pissed, he told himself. Give him more time with the Frau Sergeant-Major with tits like watermelons and a stomach like a silken pillow, plus another bit of her anatomy in which Sergeant Schulze was taking a particular interest at this moment.

Listening to the sergeant-major's speech which he had heard often enough too, von Dodenburg's interest began to wander as well. His thoughts also started to border on the carnal, as young men's thoughts will. He said to Dietz, 'Will you be needing me this afternoon, Major? I thought I'd go to the Charité and see if the medics have finally come up with some cure for my thin shits. I swear that Popov bug has scraped my gut dead clean. I don't think I could pass another turd. But . . .' He shrugged and left the subject unfinished.

Dietz turned to him, forgetting the Bull and new recruits for a moment. 'I don't know, Kuno. If I were a suspicious individual, I'd suspect that your visits to Berlin were occasioned by an interest in another orifice than the one located in the rear of your anatomy.' He laughed shortly. 'No matter, enjoy your time out of war. Let the medics look at your fart cannon, if that's what you're about. The Vulture will soon be back and then, my dear young comrade, thin shits or no thin shits, there'll be no more time for visits to Berlin.'

Von Dodenburg's smile vanished momentarily. Outside, the Bull was crying, 'Welcome to SS Assault Regiment Wotan. You are our young comrades, who will enhance the reputation of your new unit, I am sure of that . . .', as Kuno asked, 'But where is our beloved leader, Major?'

Dietz jerked at his now wooden arm and looked cautiously to left and right, as if he feared he might well be overheard. 'All I knew, Kuno, is that he has been summoned to the Führer's Eastern Headquarters. There he was to meet the Führer . . .' he hesitated momentarily, 'and someone else of great importance.'

'Who?'

'Even if I know, I wouldn't be able to tell you, Kuno. All I know is this: there's something going on and my guess is that those poor sad sacks down there will be enhancing the reputation of their new unit sooner than they think – those of them who survive.'

Up at his window, Sergeant Schulze smiled maliciously as the Bull finished off his speech of welcome with the words, 'And tonight, comrades, it will give me the greatest of pleasure to drink with you, if you wish to invite your old sergeant-major for a beer or two', and said, 'There's going to be fun and games tonight, Matzi, you Bavarian barnshitter.' He made his intention quite clear with an obscene thrust of his brawny right arm.

Matz shook his head as if he didn't understand the world any more, saying in a sombre tone, 'Some of us have no respect for their senior NCOs – and their chattels.'

To which Schulze said, 'Take it from me, old house, a stiff prick hasn't got a conscience.' And with that he immediately repaired to his own quarters and began searching for an adequate supply of what he called 'Parisians'* for the night to come.

Young Kuno von Dodenburg was enjoying himself. For the first time since the fall of France in 1940 two years before,

* SS slang for what the British soldier called 'French letters', i.e. contraceptives.

he seemed to be able to relax. Even the Iraq fiasco of the year before was forgotten,* though he was still suffering its effects in the form of what the ordinary stubble-hopper called 'thin shits', very persistent 'thin shits' indeed. Not that the ailment curbed his style. Currently he was making love to an older aristocratic lady, whose husband was serving on the staff in faraway France – 'and he can stay there with his cheap whore for the rest of the war, Kuno, as far as I'm concerned'; a youth leader in the 'League of German Maidens', who was not particularly pretty, but who possessed remarkable sexual energy – 'We German Maidens, Kuno, must be as swift as a greyhound, tough like leather and hard as Krupp steel', which she was (he often left her bruised all over); and Magda, the pathetic, hopeless widow of a young infantry officer killed in the first days of the Polish campaign back in what seemed another age, September 1939. 'Oh God,' Magda would sigh, clinging to him till it hurt, 'what shall I do without you? *Please, please*, tell me you won't leave me – *ever*.'

Kuno von Dodenburg didn't know about 'ever', but he did know that he had no intention of leaving the fleshpots of Berlin – and Magda – just yet. The Vulture, Wotan's CO, had been gone for a week now; Dietz, the acting CO, was easy-going and still shocked by having his left arm shot off in Russia; and the regiment needed all the time it could get to reorganize before it was sent to the hell of the Russian front once again. For if the harshly handsome and arrogant young SS officer was concerned with his own pleasures this autumn of 1942, he was still concerned too with the fate of SS Assault Regiment Wotan. Wotan had been wasted in combat more than once. This time Kuno was determined, if and when Wotan went into battle again, it would be fully trained and had absorbed all the tricks of this deadly business of killing from Wotan's surviving 'old hares'. Young soldiers straight from the depots could only survive if they knew those tricks of the trade. The manuals, the drill, the weapon training really meant nothing in combat; but know-

* See L. Kessler, *Operation Iraq* (Severn House) for further details.

ing when to duck, when not to open fire and, if necessary, when to do a bunk did.

Now Dietz's comment about the possibility of action sooner than the regiment anticipated made him feel that the good times were coming to an end; he had to take his pleasures while he still could; perhaps time was running out for Wotan – what else could the Vulture, the CO, be up to than finding a new assignment for them which would gain for him those general's stars that he lusted after?

'Major,' Kuno asked, as the Bull dismissed the recruits and the *Hiwis* started to drag their kit to the barracks amid jeers of 'you'll be sorry' and 'piss-pansies unite' from the watching old hares, 'I wonder if I can borrow your staff car for the afternoon when I go to see the sawbones at La Charité about my complaint.'

Dietz grinned. 'Are you sure, Kuno, that's the only complaint you're trying to get attended to this afternoon?' Without waiting for an answer, he added, 'Certainly, take it, old house. If Igor has finished polishing it, it's yours. Enjoy yourself, while you can.' He tapped his wooden arm, as if reminding himself that he was a certified cripple now, his smile vanishing. 'Off you go.'

Kuno swung the major a tremendous salute and marched out to the rear of the HQ, where Igor, their Russian *Hiwi*, was sweating hard as he polished the pre-war Horch, the sweat glistening on his round Mongol face.

'*Boshe moi*,' Kuno said in Russian, 'you'll wear it away, if you keep polishing it like that. Besides it's due for another coat of camouflage paint soon.'

'*Horoscho*,' Iger paused and came to attention, as if he were a fully fledged member of Wotan, instead of a former Red Army man who had turned up in their lines in Russia, hands held high above his shaven head, crying the only words of German that he had known at that time, 'I surrender . . . Kamerad, I surrender . . .'

'Town,' von Dodenburg ordered and opened the door of the big tourer.

Igor bowed, as if he were some flunky used to the ways of

the aristocracy. He straightened up and in that instant von Dodenburg could have sworn the roly-poly Russian winked as he said, 'Hospital for shits?'

'Yes, hospital for shits,' von Dodenburg agreed and dismissed the driver, as he watched Schulze and his running mate, Matz, leaving the gate in front of him, obviously without a pass, for the two rogues were handing something which looked like a flatman of schnaps to the guard commander. Kuno shook his head and told himself that the two of them were up to no good, as usual, but then, he thought, neither was he.

Two

Central Berlin was as hectic as ever. The troop trains were arriving and departing for the East Front once again and the streets leading up to the Charité were filled with hysterical, happy, sobbing, laughing women and children waving cheap swastika flags at their arriving and departing menfolk, who seemed bewildered by all the fuss. Laden like pack animals, watched as always by the hard-eyed 'chained-up dogs', the military police, on the lookout for deserters and those who intended to become one soon, they stared open-mouthed at the scene.

All the same, despite the banners proclaiming new victories in the East and the booming loudspeakers recording the huge numbers of Red Army prisoners taken and equipment destroyed this week, the ordinary Berliners seemed shabbier than ever. Undernourished men and women, heads buried in the collars of their threadbare coats, hurried past the still smoking ruins of the previous night's RAF bombing raid, while ancient wood-burning open trucks and the odd taxi packed with earnest-looking businessmen with their imitation briefcases, looked straight ahead as if they didn't want to register what had happened to their home town in these last terrible months of total aerial warfare.

'*Im Raume Charkov*,' the loudspeakers echoed and re-echoed, '*Einheiten der Waffen SS schlugen einen feindlichen Gegenangriff zuruck. Die Verluste des Feindes waren sehr hoch—*'

Igor, behind the wheel of the stalled car, tired of hooting his horn at the crowds hindering his progress, beamed and shouted to von Dodenburg beside him, 'Our boys . . . dey show those goddam Popovs eh, *Hauptsturmbannführer*? The Popovs – they cannot bear our boys.'

If he hadn't been so impatient, Kuno would have laughed out loud. A Russian ex-POW praising his captors as 'our boys'. Instead he said, 'All right, Igor. I'll get out here. You take the car back straightaway. *Ponemyu*?' As always Kuno, like the other veterans of the Russian front, interspersed his German with Russian words; the old hares even did it with each other.

'*Ponemyu*,' Igor said smartly, as Kuno opened the Horch's door and pushed his way through the crowd, but as the SS officer disappeared the happy smile vanished from Igor's broad Mongolian face to be replaced by a look of earnest deliberation; it was that of a man who suddenly felt himself confronted by a serious problem.

Von Dodenburg turned the corner. Up ahead lay Berlin's most famous hospital, La Charité. The street leading to it was packed with wounded soldiers clad in the blue-and-white pyjamas of the wounded. Whatever had happened to them in the past, now they were happy, laughing and joking, happy to have escaped the Russian front. To von Dodenburg's right, an old woman in ill-fitting men's tweed trousers, tied around the waist with a piece of rope, was carefully picking up the cigarette ends tossed away by the young men under a sign reading, '*We Thank Thee, Our Führer*'. She saw von Dodenburg looking at her and winked knowingly in the fashion of a much younger woman. 'Thank him, we can, sir,' she said in her thick cheeky Berlin accent. 'Without him we wouldn't have had all this.' She indicated the ruins all around.

As an SS officer, Kuno von Dodenburg knew he should have reprimanded her for her cheek and the insult to the Führer. But his mood was too good; he hadn't the heart to do so. So he winked back at the ugly old crone and said, 'You can say that again, granny,' tossing her his own half-smoked cigarette as he did so.

'Welcome to the slaughterhouse, von Dodenburg,' Professor Martens of the La Charité gave him his usual ironic greeting as he entered the hospital's big airy consulting room, the customary 'sample' in his hand. 'Still shitting copiously, I wonder.'

Martens, a big bald man, clad in the usual white robe over his colonel's uniform, the habitual cynical smile on his well-nourished face, indicated that von Dodenburg should sit down, saying, 'I don't think I'll offer you my hand, if you don't mind.'

Kuno played his game, for he liked the doctor who had been his own father's regimental surgeon back in the trenches in the 'old war'. 'Well, if I were you, sir, I wouldn't do so either.'

'Quite so. Well, you're improving. The strain is weakening and I suppose in other circumstances I might well be able to clear you for active service once more.'

The statement puzzled Kuno. He asked, 'I don't quite follow, sir. What circumstances?'

'Well . . .' Martens hesitated and lowered his voice, 'if I didn't think the circumstances indicate that the balloon might well go up again once more. I mean, I have a duty to your old father as well, you know.'

Kuno understood. 'You mean as a favour to him, you want to keep me on the sick list. But sir, I see no sign of trouble on the horizon to the east. Winter's already on its way on the Russian front and "General Frost" will certainly rule in the East. We can't cope with the mud and the frost and the damned sub-zero temperatures out there.'

The old colonel, whose shock of white hair that was his beard contrasted strangely with his bald pate, frowned a little. 'I don't know about that, young man, but what I do know is this. We have been ordered to upgrade as fit again for active service all lightly wounded men, especially if they are infantry. You're armoured infantry, indeed one of the best. Do you want to go to the front again? I mean I could keep you here another three months, if you wish, till whatever happens is over.' He cocked his wise old head to one side and looked at the younger man in that cynical, quizzical manner of his. 'You might be able to enjoy life for a further – well, you know what I mean,' he added hastily as there was a tap on the door of his office.

'*Herein*,' he snapped with the full authority of his rank and medical title.

It was Captain Doctor Hausser, a thin bitter man who was in charge of the great hospital's VD wards – 'the only doctor in La Charité who washes his hands *before* he urinates,' as the old colonel was wont to quip. He clicked to attention momentarily, nodded to von Dodenburg and said, 'In three devils' name, why did God ever invent cunt? There must have been some other less dangerous way of reproducing the species.'

Martens fluttered his beard and, smiling a little, said, 'Life would be very boring without it, Hausser, eh? It's the carrot that keeps the donkey going. How would we spend our spare time otherwise?'

'As far as the *Wehrmacht* is concerned,' Hausser persisted, obviously not listening to the old colonel, 'syphilis means the loss of a fighting soldier for thirty-seven days and gonorrhoea for twenty-nine. So they try to keep our soldiers clean by having brothels at the front. But wayward idle creatures that those front swine are, they go looking elsewhere for their sexual pleasures. The result—'

'. . . is,' Martens beat the irate captain to it, 'that you have a nice cushy speciality here at La Charité.'

'Admittedly, but I take my job seriously, sir. So what am I to do, I ask you, when the authorities order me to pump my unfortunates full of sulpha drugs and send them back to the front uncured, probably passing on their loathsome diseases to some innocent German women on the way there.'

Martens's cynical mood vanished. 'This is news to me,' he snapped.

'It almost looks, sir, that they are weeding out anyone who can walk and fire a rifle. Colleagues tell me that they are forming special battalions of infantrymen who have been deafened in action and those whose guts mean they have to eat a special diet.' He shook his head in mock wonder. 'It can't go on, sir. It must be stopped and I think you as a senior officer and experienced medical specialist ought—'

'To do something about it,' Martens cut him off once again.

'Yes, I understand. I'll talk to Professor Sauerbruch and see what he says.* Thank you.'

The Professor waited till the angry VD specialist had left before turning to von Dodenburg, who was half-amused and half-puzzled by the interchange, and saying, 'You see. That proves what I have just said. They're clearing the hospital. Why? Because there's a new offensive on the way and you, my dear young man, ought not to take part in it. You've risked your life often enough. Besides, you've cured your throatache.' He indicated the bright, shining medal of the Knight's Cross hanging from Kuno's throat. 'Do you want more honours? They won't do you much good when you're dead, eh?'

Kuno felt abruptly angry and at the same time uneasy. For a while in these last weeks, he felt he had managed to gain control over his life and enjoy himself, no longer worried overly much about Germany and the fate of the regiment. Now it seemed he was losing control; circumstances – the shitting war – were taking over again. 'I think, sir, you're overreacting,' he said.

'Am I? Why?'

'Why? Because, sir, our Führer would not do something so foolish as to attack in Russia in the depth of winter. We got a bloody nose last winter when we did so. I think we've learned our lesson, to wait till spring before we attack again.'

'You think so, eh?' The old colonel looked at the suddenly flushed Kuno cynically. 'A long time ago, young man, when I was a medical student at Heidelberg before the old war, we had a saying when we were dealing with the frailities of humanity. It went something like this.' He frowned and then said, as the memory of that long-forgotten phrase came back to him, '"Out of the crooked timber of humanity nothing straight was ever made." I think the quip came from Kant. I think, whatever you say to the contrary, that is still our position today.'

Kuno's frown deepened. As young as he was, he didn't take to being lectured even when the lecturer had his interests at heart as an old friend of his father, the general.

* A famous surgeon at La Charité at the time.

'We see it daily here at La Charité.' Suddenly the old colonel looked angry. 'Here where everything should be straight and orderly, nothing is. The whole structure of one of our most famous hospitals is bent – corrupt. From top to bottom. Our orderlies pinch the wounded's rations and sell them on the black market. The doctors do the same with the drugs. Even the famous Sauerbruch compromises himself, *not* for what he does, but for what he *doesn't* do. The whole damned lot of us are rotten to the core.'

'But what has this got to do with the supposed winter offensive, sir?' Kuno interrupted as the old colonel's eyes blazed with anger, his chest heaving a little with the effort of speaking so much. 'And me for that matter, too?'

'Why? I'll tell you, young man. Why should you risk your life for a corrupt system and I don't just mean here at La Charité?' Even in his anger, the old colonel lowered his voice in case anyone else was listening and reported him to the Gestapo. 'As long as brave fools like you continue to fight at the front for your country and a bit of cheap enamel to hang round your necks, you will help to perpetuate a crooked system. People like you will unwittingly assist in plunging our country deeper into the morass. Let you heroes stay at home and take the backbone out of the front. Let the front be manned by the second-raters, cowards, potential deserters, criminals from the penal battalions. They value their own lives first and their country second. If the Führer starts a winter offensive, and I think he will – he believes it is his destiny to win in the end—'

'Sir,' Kuno protested, 'don't talk like this. Walls have ears. There could be trouble . . .' His words trailed away to nothing. The old colonel wasn't listening.

'They'll break and run. That will see the start of the end. The collapse of a regime that will destroy our beloved Germany. We still have a chance to save the Fatherland. The future belongs to brave men like you, Kuno. We need you alive and not a dead hero at the front—' He stopped abruptly, his rage vanishing as swiftly as it had come, and stared at von Dodenburg, as if he were seeing him for the very first time.

'Sir,' Kuno said carefully. 'I appreciate your concern. But it is misplaced, if I may say so. I don't think there can be a winter offensive. The hospitals are being cleared to prepare the men for a spring offensive, which is very likely.' He shrugged. 'But whenever Germany attacks, I must be part of that attack. The von Dodenburgs have served Prussia and Germany for over two hundred years ever since the time of Old Fritz. They have never cared much whether their political masters of the time were right or wrong. First came duty and loyalty and, if necessary, death for the sake of the Fatherland.' Kuno von Dodenburg was surprised at his own words and how articulate he was. He took a deep breath and continued with, 'Thank you very much for your efforts on my behalf, *Herr Professor*. I appreciate them and I am sure my father does too. But if I am called to fight this winter, which I don't think I will be, I shall go back to the front, thin shits or no thin shits.' He attempted to grin at his use of the soldiers' crude expression for his complaint; it would lighten this sudden confrontation, he thought.

It didn't. Professor Martens opened his mouth and, thinking better of it, said no more. Instead, he pulled a sheet of his personal notepaper from the rack and scribbed on it very fast with his fountain pen. Finished, he thrust it at Kuno. 'Take it if you wish, Herr von Dodenburg,' he said very formally, though his voice was not completely under control. 'It's your medical discharge from La Charité. I am passing you on to your own battalion medical officer. He'll take care of you from now on.' He bent his bald head over his papers, the tears falling silently on the first sheet. Awkwardly Kuno clicked his heels together and saluted. The professor didn't seem to notice. The young SS officer went out, his shoulders bent as if in defeat.

Three

If Kuno von Dodenburg's mood had changed from happy to sombre that autumn afternoon in Berlin, Sergeant-Major Bulle's had been changed in the opposite direction. His customary hard, harsh mood had been transformed by the arrival of the new recruits with their pockets full of their first pay as trained soldiers: innocent greenbeaks who would be only too eager to buy their dear old sergeant-major several litres of suds, which would be washed down by his favourite schnaps before they'd fight to buy him a black-market blowout of *Eisbein und Sauerkraut*.

Strengthened by the suds and *Sauerkraut*, he would return to his married quarters where his beloved wife, Hannelore, would be waiting for him on the sofa under their portrait of the Führer, dutifully knitting socks for the men at the front, as all decent German women should, where he would oblige her by slipping her a length of genuine German salami that undoubtedly would make her eyeballs pop.

Now as he attached the ribbon of the Iron Cross, Second Class, to his tunic and fixed his marksman's lanyard so that it hung correctly from his shoulder, he looked at Hannelore lovingly, wondering whether he should give her a free feel now before he went out; it might well get her in the right mood for later if he put his hand up her skirt right now as she sprawled on the sofa, legs spread wide, eating chocolate after chocolate from a box that she had obtained somewhere or other. How, he didn't know; for chocolates cost a fortune on Berlin's black market.

Just as he was about to make his decision to give his plump young wife the kind of pleasure that would make her forget her chocolates, she said, her mouth full of strawberry praline, 'And I don't want yer coming back pissed and thinking yer gonna put that dirty thing of yours inside me after I've had a bath. 'Cos yer not. A woman's got to have a bit of sleep now and then. We're different from you great oafs of men. We haven't got our brains between our legs, yer know.' She swallowed her strawberry praline and reached immediately for another one, her fingers circling the almost empty box delicately till she found the one that took her fancy.

'But my little cheetah—' he began.

She cut him off immediately. 'None of that little cheetah crap,' she snapped, her mouth full again. 'You've had your ration for this month last Sunday and that's that.' She jerked her legs, and his heart nearly stopped beating. He could see that she wasn't wearing any knickers. His face flushed angrily, as if he were about to 'make a sow' of some unfortunate soldier on the parade ground. *Who in three devils' name does she think she is?* an irate little voice at the back of his head demanded. *After all, she is married to a sergeant-major of the Waffen SS and living a life of luxury. Yet she is refusing me what is rightfully mine – by law. I've got a licence to prove it.* He opened his mouth to shout at her but changed his mind at the very last moment. He thought of the suds and fodder – *for nothing* – which shortly would lie before him. When he came home he'd show her who was master here. She'd open them legs of hers for him whether she liked it or not.

'I won't bother to kiss you,' he said ironically, 'with all that chocolate in yer mouth.' He made a final adjustment to his cap, setting it to a slightly rakish angle – for a sergeant-major.

'Kiss me,' she sneered. 'That'll be the day.' As if to emphasize her contempt for him, she spread her plump legs even wider and scratched her hairy pubes.

He swallowed hard and decided he'd better go at once. '*Tschuss*,' he said. 'Don't wait up for me, if you don't want to.'

She didn't even bother to reply. Instead, she continued to scratch her pubic hairs and with her free hand searched for yet another chocolate.

From the window of his barrack-room, Schulze watched

the Bull's progress across the square, sternly returning the salutes of the recruits, most of them scared out of their wits at the sight of the sergeant-major bearing down upon them. 'Hey shit,' Matz at his side exclaimed, 'he looks like Jesus walking across the water.'

Schulze guffawed at the thought of what was to come this night. 'He might – at the moment, Matzi. But he's gonna fall into it before this night is out, believe you me.'

Matzi frowned and looked worried suddenly. 'You are frigging chancing your arm, Schulzi. If he catches you, he's bound to have you shipped to Torgau* before yer feet touch the ground.'

'He'll have to get up earlier in the morning if he's gonna catch Frau Schulze's handsome son, Matzi.'

'But why bother with her? I don't think you'll find much fun in rattling her bones.'

'It's not fun I'm after,' Schulze answered. 'I'm taking revenge. That big bugger has got away with murder too often. He needs to be taken down a peg or two. Wait till the regiment finds out that while the sergeant-major was getting pissed on free beer blackmailed out of the greenbeaks, some rascal, whose name I cannot reveal, has been slipping his fat missus a length or two on his very own couch in his very own quarters. The Bull'll never live it down.'

'If you say so, Schulzi,' Matz said, unconvinced, 'but frigging well watch yer step. He's a bad bastard that Bull.'

Schulze laughed, and down below, the *Hiwi* known as Igor smiled as if in approval, his mind racing in the attempt to use what might happen this night to his own advantage . . .

So far it had been a fine party, the Bull told himself, as he picked his teeth to get the remains of the *Eisbein und Sauerkraut* out, belching at regular intervals like some desert Arab showing his approval of a rare feast. His 'boys', as he was calling the green recruits, had done him well. The beer and the schnaps chasers had flowed mightily, the *Eisbein und*

* Notorious military prison.

Sauerkraut had come in such a huge portion that the establishment's strongest waiter had required assistance from his colleagues to carry it.

Naturally the 'boys' had been unable to hold their suds. It was what he had expected of them. Several lay unconscious on the wooden benches, resting their heads in pools of stale beer. One was hanging from the umbrella stand by the collar of his tunic, snoring happily. Another was asking old 'Auntie Hedwig', the place's raddled old whore, who had had more soldiers up her knickers than had taken part in the invasion of Poland back in '39, if she would marry him. Naturally, the greenbeak had said with drunken solemnity, he'd have to get her mother's permission. This the Bull thought very funny, seeing as the whore's mother had won the Iron Cross, Third Class, for servicing a company of infantry badly shaken after the Battle of Verdun in the Old War.

Yes, the Bull kept reminding himself, he was drunk and happy. All he needed to round off a very successful evening was to dance the mattress polka with Hannelore. He simply couldn't get her ample charms out of his befuddled brain, especially that last sight of that hairy thing of hers as she had lolled on the sofa with her plump thighs spread. A little poke at that, he reasoned, would do him nicely. He'd sleep like a log afterwards. He belched and nodded to one of the recruits to fetch him some more good Bavarian suds.

But the big brutal-looking sergeant-major was not fated to enjoy his Hannelore this particular evening. For he was half way through a fresh litre of Munich beer when he heard the commotion outside. At first he paid little attention to the noise. In the taverns and bars around the barracks, there was always trouble late at night, especially when the soldiers got paid. Most of the recruits couldn't hold their beer and there were usually fights and brawls, especially between different or rival battalions. The 'chained-up dogs', the military police, would soon sort out the problem, the Bull reasoned.

But this time the chained-up dogs didn't make an appearance and the noise seemed to be getting louder. Indeed the shaven-headed landlord, unlit cigarette stump stuck between his gold teeth, rubber hose in his right hand, cursed and started to open the door to where the recruits were holding their drunken 'smoker'. It was then that a suddenly startled Bull heard that all too familiar voice, declaring, '*Was fur einen Saustall!* What kind of drunken piggery is this . . . and my Wotan too . . . Heaven, arse and cloudburst, who's in charge here?'

The Bull knew who was in charge and he knew, too, what would happen to him if he was found here, a senior NCO in charge of a bunch of hopelessly drunken recruits. For someone so large and so drunk, he reacted swiftly. In the same instant that the familiar figure, dressed in civilian clothes and accompanied by a pretty young man with a slightly powdered face, came through the door, he crashed through the door of the latrine and was crawling through the place's rear window like some raw recruit himself, muttering fearfully, 'Holy straw-sack, *it's the Vulture*!'

Sergeant Schulze acted with equal speed as he heard the heavy boots slogging their way drunkenly ever the gravel outside Hannelore's married quarters. The sergeant-major's plump wife was naked save for her black lace bra which Bull had bought her once in Paris, sprawled under the portrait of the Führer, panting as if she were in the throes of some final attack of asthma, while Schulze, his body lathered in sweat, pumped away with all his strength, feeling somehow that he might as well be inflating a large barrage balloon. For Hannelore was taking all the time in the world, although she knew her husband would be coming home soon. Now here he was and a suddenly alarmed Schulze knew what would happen to him if the sergeant-major caught him in his present state.

Rapidly he withdrew himself with a loud sucking noise, as Hannelore gasped, her eyes tightly screwed up, 'Just one more stroke, beloved . . . and I'll come.'

'And I'm going,' he hissed, grabbing for his trousers, which were hanging by their braces from the Führer's portrait. 'It's your old man.'

'*Nein*, *nein*!' she cried, grabbing at his arms frantically. 'I'm coming. Don't let me down . . . That one stroke.'

Desperate, hearing those big boots of Bull's coming ever closer, Schulze thrust his loins forward with all his brute strength. She shrieked with delight. 'I've come,' she exclaimed as the Führer's portrait collapsed on top of her.

Schulze grabbed for his trousers and fled naked into the blackout, crying over his shoulder as he did, 'Get yer knickers on, woman . . . Quick! It'll make you look more respectable, showing all yer whereabouts like that,' and then he was gone, running for his life.

In his quarters, unable to sleep, von Dodenburg smoked moodily, watching the spectral moon scud in and out of the clouds. His good mood of the last days had vanished completely. Even the reassuring steady pace of the sentries outside on the hard gravel path could not restore his feeling of order and that everything was well with the world.

That evening he could have slept with the decadent aristocrat with her sexual fantasies and wishes which were very far advanced for a woman barely out of her teens. But he hadn't felt the desire and he had turned her down even though she had offered to bring her 'good friend' who was 'an absolutely wonderful fuck' to join them in a threesome.

Thus he stood there now, a tall young man with a harshly handsome face, whittled down to the bone with the last two years of the war, staring at the moon and listening to the drunken singing of the recruits returning to their barracks before the midnight curfew came into force.

Not for long though.

Suddenly, startlingly, there was chaos in the barracks, which had already settled down for the night. At the gate he heard the sharp command of the guard commander crying, 'Fall in, the guard . . . Officer approaching!' On the square a bugler appeared, doing up his tunic with frantic fingers to commence playing 'Officer call', with more urgency than normal. Everywhere, lights flashed on in the barracks to be covered the next moment with the blackout screens. Heavy boots ran to and fro.

Next moment, as the guard commander ordered, 'Commanding Officer – present arms!', Dietz came hurtling through the door, totally naked and dripping water as if he had just taken a shower, to announce, 'I'm pissed as anything. Now he's here, totally out of the blue and wanting all officers to attend him in fifteen minutes on the nose. What a frigging mess!' He ran his hand through his wet, tousled, blond locks.

'Who's here?' von Dodenburg barked above the racket outside, shaken out of his reverie immediately.

'The Vulture . . . the frigging Vulture and he's out for blood . . .'

Four

The Vulture had not enjoyed the long ride through the silent Russian forest one bit. He knew from what he had heard at the Führer's Eastern Front HQ that Russian partisans had penetrated this far west and he had no wish to fall into those savages' hands. He knew what his fate would be as a colonel in the SS: a cruel lingering death with no mercy shown. Admittedly he had an escort of four cavalryman under the command of a young lieutenant who displayed an interesting bottom in his tight, tailor-made breeches.

But he guessed the five of them wouldn't be much use against a determined attack by the partisans, or, even worse, by marauding Cossack patrols, who were even more cruel.

Still, the mysterious German general who was in charge of Intelligence had ordered that this would be the way they met – 'We cannot even trust our own people at the Führer HQ, Colonel' – and so this was the manner in which the conference was going to be held.

The Vulture stroked the monstrous nose which had given him his nickname in SS Assault Regiment Wotan and cursed the General, who was risking his life in this way, allowing his hand to slip down to his pistol holster and burying himself once again in a cocoon of his own thoughts and apprehensions; they weren't nice.

Time passed. The only sound now was the clip-clop of their horses' hooves in the tracks and the mournful howl of an owl a long way off. They might have been the last men left alive on the earth. The handsome young lieutenant with the tight breeches spurred his mount closer to that of the SS colonel and whispered, though there seemed no reason to do, 'Not much further, *Obersturmbannführer*. We have to keep an eye peeled for a red flashing light. That is the signal.'

The Vulture grunted something and loosened his pistol in its holster even more. God knows, he told himself, anything could happen in this arsehole of the world. Still, it seemed that the Führer had a hand in this mysterious business personally, and he knew that with the Führer there could be no arguments. Besides, whatever it was all about, if it brought him closer to those general's stars which he craved for as much as those delightful, powdered, young, pretty boys, it would be worth it.

Five minutes later the young adjutant at his side spotted the red light, the signal, winking off and on through the trees and then they were riding towards the dark silhouette of a half-ruined castle of the type favoured by the Junkers, who had once ruled this part of the world.

The Vulture breathed a sigh of relief as he spotted the sentries and a machine-gun post dug in and manned at the side of the long drive leading up to the place, from which came the faint hum of electricity and what seemed to be high-speed Morse, indicating that it was occupied and busy even at this time of the night. Soon, he told himself, he'd find out what all this damned hocus-pocus was about.

The Vulture was to be disappointed. The mystery was not to be explained just yet. Indeed what happened next appeared only to deepen it.

The young officer with the delightfully tight riding breeches ushered him into a large room that smelled of decay and neglect, where a private soldier was waiting for them, complete with what appeared to be a film projector. 'There you are, sir.' The officer, bowing from the waist and extending his right hand like some head waiter ushering in some favoured guest who tipped well, indicated an easy chair with, next to it, a small table upon which rested a box of cigars and what looked a collection of *piccolos*.* 'Please help yourself, sir.'

* Small bottles of German champagne. *Transl.*

The Vulture grunted something but didn't vent his anger and frustration on the young officer; he was too pretty for that. Instead he opened a piccolo and poured its ice-cold contents into a tall champagne glass while, behind him, the officer spoke in whispers to the man at the projector. Their conversation seemed to go on for ages and in frustration, the Vulture lit one of the cigars, knowing instinctively he wasn't going to see anyone of importance just yet.

He was right.

Suddenly there was a click. The room went dark. He nearly upset his glass of German *Sekt*. 'What—' he began, but already the screen in front him started to flicker with light. A voice spoke in Russian. Before him, a film began to roll. It showed what was obviously a pre-war Russian city. Happy citizens bustled to and fro. There were shots of buildings, mostly ancient, but all of them bearing slogans in Russian, probably advocating the virtues of the 'Workers' and Peasants'' state. Despite his shock at this sudden film performance, the Vulture was intrigued. What in three devils' name was he being shown this film for?

A moment later he started to guess why. For the film had changed abruptly. The happy-looking workers and peasants vanished suddenly. They were replaced by grim-faced soldiers in Red Army uniform marching through the unknown Russian city. They were followed by what appeared to be an artillery bombardment. The gracious eighteenth-century buildings, set along the banks of a great river, started to tumble down in great clouds of dust and masonry.

The pace increased dramatically. Civilians, clad in rags, had been photographed. They staggered joltingly, continued a few paces and fell face forward in the snow, not to move again. Horror upon horror. Now the bodies of those haggard civilians lay unattended in the icy gutters. Others were stacked up on the sidewalk like piles of logs. Stukas came tumbling out of winter skies to unload their deadly steel eggs on the running civilians below. More and more of them . . . and the shattered buildings disappeared in furious flames and clouds of smoke.

The noise of the bombing and the wail of sirens was replaced by that of emaciated babies, eyes bulging out of starving, skull-like faces as they attempted to suckle breasts that were flaccid, wrinkled and devoid of milk. Men and women scraped off wallpaper and steamed the back to remove the paste, with which they appeared to be making a kind of gruel to feed other starving children . . .

The Vulture, who had no sympathy or understanding of these starving Russians, felt now he had seen enough. He wondered, too, why he, the commander of an SS battalion, which had fought in Russia, should be subjected to the picture. He knew what was going on in Russia, didn't he? All that interested him about the strange film show was why had he been brought here to see it and what was the name of the Russian city which appeared to have suffered so much – and for such a long time. For the dreadful scenes depicted took place both over winter and summer. But for the life of him, the Vulture couldn't identify any Russian city which had been under attack that long, not even Moscow. He opened another *piccolo* and waited for the strange film to end and enlightenment.

It came in just the same surprising way as the movie itself. Abruptly the film ended just as startingly as it had begun. A voice boomed, 'Obersturmbannführer Geier.'

'Yes.' He turned around swiftly, trying to ascertain where the voice had come from. But there was no one to be seen in the glowing darkness save the private soldier and the handsome young cavalry officer. 'What the devil's going on?' he demanded, at the end of his patience. 'What kind of damn-fool game is this?'

The unknown voice didn't answer his questions directly. Instead it continued in that metallic booming fashion with, 'Since we captured that film, things have got much worse in the city. They are now eating a jelly made from carpenter's glue. The dead are left unburied for days and it is said that cannibalism is rife. People are going out at night and sawing off the tender bits of the dead to eat.'

The voice paused and let the Vulture absorb the information.

By now his brain was in a whirl. First this strange place, then the film and now this authoritarian disembodied voice filling him in with information that seemed to have no relevance for him. If he only knew where this place in Russia was and what concern it was of SS Assault Regiment Wotan, then he could commence thinking straight.

But the voice was not going to grant him that wish just yet. It continued with, 'We feel now that the city is ripe for the taking. Even the infantry who are bearing the brunt of our attacks are on half-rations and as you know, *Obersturmbannführer*, no Ivan fights without his daily ration of vodka. But there is no vodka and the infantry are looting the warehouses containing the dried orange rind intended for the city's infants and are making some sort of firewater out of that. In short it is five minutes to eleven for the city and its defenders.'

The information that the end of the city was nigh gave the Vulture the opportunity he was waiting for to ask that overwhelming question. 'But what city is this?' he asked swiftly.

The voice seemed to hesitate. Then it announced quite solemnly, 'Leningrad!'

The Vulture caught his breath. Leningrad, the city once known as St Petersburg, built by the legendary Peter the Great himself and named after him until the communists had taken over at the end of Great War. Everyone knew it was a prestige object for German arms. Renamed after the first communist leader Lenin, Stalin, the current communist dictator, was defending the city with all his might. For his part, the Führer was equally determined to capture the place. Now he realized that Wotan was going to play some part in the German attack on Leningrad. What, he couldn't imagine, but he guessed he would be soon enlightened on the subject; and he realized, too, that it would be a very special role. Why else this mystery and the meeting in this remote place?

Half an hour later, after he had half eaten a meal (for he was too excited to be interested in the rather splendid food that a white-tunicked military waiter had set before him), he finally met his host, the possessor of the voice.

He was a medium-sized general with the crimson stripe of the Greater German General Staff running down the side of his trousers. His face was clever-looking but hard with intelligent, sharp eyes that seemed to dart everywhere and take in everything, and the Vulture could see from the lack of decorations on the skinny general's chest that he had seen little frontline action. The general was one of those the Wotan troopers called 'rear-echelon stallions'.

'Obersturmbannführer Geier,' the general snapped, 'my name is Gehlen. Commander of Foreign Armies East.'

Geier clicked his heels and gave the general a stiff Prussian bow from the waist. He had heard of this mysterious general who commanded all of German Intelligence in the East. He was never photographed, he had heard, and wherever he had to make an appearance at the Führer's Headquarters to give a briefing Gehlen insisted that only senior officers should be present and he should never be quizzed by anyone less than the Führer afterwards. Gehlen, it seemed, was an officer who had played the intelligence game with his cards held tightly to his chest.

Gehlen indicated that the Vulture should sit down again. He said, 'Please smoke,' and then without even waiting for the younger officer to reach for his cigarettes, as if he were a man who had no time whatsoever for social graces, he said, 'In exactly one month's time, Obersturmbannführer Geier, you will lead your battalion in an attack on Leningrad. This is at the Führer's express wish and –' he glanced keenly at the Vulture, as if he were trying to detect any weakness in the latter's ugly face, dominated by that great beak of a nose – 'he doesn't expect you to fail. Now let me tell you the plan . . .'

Five

'*Meine Herren*,' the Vulture barked, still very angry at the sight of so many drunken Wotan troopers earlier on, '*wir haben einen Auftrag . . . Von dem Führer selbst*.'

Despite their tiredness, the overindulgence of the evening, the news electrified the officers assembled in the smoke-filled mess, which had been cleared of mess waiters, cooks and the like; for the fact that Wotan had been given a mission by the Führer personally had to be limited to officers only.

'I cannot give you many details at this moment. But I say this. We march in one month's time and we will march on Leningrad.'

Again the assembled officers started at the mention of the Russian city which had been under siege since the summer and where the *Wehrmacht* had suffered tremendous casualties in successive attacks. For his part von Dodenburg told himself that Professor Martens of La Charité had been right. They were combing the hospital to weed out more bodies for a winter offensive. But what could the attackers achieve? Even with more troops, the Russian 'General Frost' would still defeat them as he had defeated previous German winter attacks.

Dietz put his thoughts into words. 'But sir,' he queried, 'how can we win a winter battle under the conditions pertaining in Russia, where our cannon freeze up and the diesel in our tanks solidifies? Not to speak of the miseries suffered by our stubble-hoppers.'

The Vulture looked at his second-in-command contemptuously. 'Who cares about such problems? Our weapons and tanks can be improved. As for our panzer grenadiers they'll have to become as hardy as their Popov opponents. And that reminds me, Dietz. Since I have been away, our men seem to have become a disorderly rabble.'

Dietz flushed, but the frustrated and angry Vulture was not going to let it go at that. Focusing on unfortunate Dietz stonily through his monocle, he continued with: 'I demand an immediate tightening of discipline. The whole regiment, and that includes the officer corps, will be confined to barracks forthwith when off duty. And mark my words, gentlemen, those cardboard soldiers of ours will be only too glad to stay and rest after the kind of daytime training I intend to subject them to.' He let his threat sink in and went on to warn them, 'I cannot give you too many details of what this new mission entails, gentlemen – I shall inform you of it bit by bit on a need to know basis – but I can tell you this here and now. The mission has a top-secret classification. Any one revealing what he knows of it to any unauthorized person will be arrested and subjected to an immediate courtmartial. In the most grave cases the sentence of that courtmartial can be only *death*!'

He swung his stony glare around the room, taking in every face in a manner that made some of the younger officers pale. 'I hope that is clear. *Death*! . . . All right, Dietz, dismiss the officers.' Without another word, he turned and stalked away, leaving the mess wreathed in silence for a few moments.

Then, slowly and solemnly, shoulders bowed slightly like condemned men, the officers started to disperse, going their separate ways in silence, each one wreathed in a cocoon of his own doubts and fears.

Kuno von Dodenburg, for his part, wasn't afraid of the Vulture and his threats; he had heard them before. Besides, two years of combat in half a dozen countries had convinced him that his luck wouldn't hold out for ever; he wouldn't outlast the war. Yet whatever his personal fate was to be, either at the hands of the enemy or even his own people, he was concerned still with the honour of his family name and now, more importantly, with that of SS Assault Regiment Wotan. The Vulture, pervert that he was, cynical of the creed of the

'New Germany', a member of the SS only because it meant rapid advancement, could never be allowed to sully Wotan's reputation for his own purposes. As he returned to his quarters and unbuckled his pistol belt, tossing it on to a chair, he swore a little oath to himself.

He returned to his bed. But although it was way after midnight and he knew that the Vulture would now have the Battalion out at six in the morning in accordance with the new regime he had threatened the officers with, he couldn't sleep. His soul rebelled at the hardness and brutalization which the Vulture had promised for the next month so that the men could die for him in this strange mission. But for what? Primarily so that the Vulture could win his damned general's stars.

'Damnit,' he cursed to himself in the manner of lonely men who converse with themselves. According to people like his father, the General, and his old friend Colonel Professor Martens, there were greater, more urgent decisions to be taken in this Germany of 1942. The country was being run by madmen who would destroy the Fatherland if they weren't stopped. Yet Kuno believed in the same creed as they did, the new young Germany which revitalized an old Europe dominated by yesterday's decrepit men. Deal with the Führer and his followers and what would be left?

No, his loyalty had to be with Wotan. Family, honour, even the Fatherland, run by criminals and madmen, all had gone. The regiment remained and a man had to have some kind of faith to cling to. In the end he fell into a troubled sleep in which the Vulture, naked and with an enormous erection, chased a squad of equally naked greenbeaks, their faces greased with sweat, as if with vaseline, while to their front a silent battalion of Ivans, wearing fur hats adorned with new snow, were waiting solemnly to shoot them down . . .

Sergeant-Major Bulle, known as the 'Bull', couldn't sleep either. At three that morning he squatted his enormous bulk in the WC of his quarters, adorned with a picture, stolen from some inn of other, of a little boy piddling into a pool, with the old legend below it, warning, '*Don't drink water. Kids piss in water.*'

But the Bull had no eyes for the beer advert. He was more concerned with his stomach, which was rumbling like an artillery battery in full action, giving off weird gurgling sounds like water gushing down a drain. '*Scheiss Eisbein*,' he cursed the pig's knuckle and *Sauerkraut* to which the greenbeaks had treated him in the inn. He sweated, his face contorted with pain. He felt he might explode at any moment. If only he could let a really juicy fart rip and get the wind out of his tortured guts he might feel much better.

Of course Hannelore, snoring loudly in the bedroom opposite, had showed no sympathy when he had awakened her to moan, 'I've got a terrible gutache, little mother.' He had pulled her gently towards him, as if she were some kind of human water bottle; her generous buttocks, all that warm naked white flesh, might well ease his pain. 'Get yer frigging nasty paws off my arse,' she had growled and jerked herself away from him, not before he had made a little discovery that troubled him now, even at this moment of acute abdominal pain.

Hannelore had been wearing the expensive black frillies which he had brought her back from conquered Paris in 1940 and which they reserved for 'special occasions' when his 'little mother' spoiled him in bed, such as on his birthday (though for some reason she had forgotten to do so on his last birthday – she had muttered something about as drunk as he was, he couldn't 'get a stiff un even if he had Sarah Leander and Maria Rokk dancing naked in front of him').

As the pain eased momentarily, the Bull said, 'Now when I left she had no knickers on and when I come back, she had – the black frillies for specials.' He addressed the naked little boy urinating mischievously into the village pond. 'Now what do you make of that, eh?'

But the naughty little boy sending a stream of yellow liquid into the water that no one in his right mind should drink, according to the brewers, could give him no answer to that overwhelming question. Next moment another spasm racked his big body, with the beads of sweat standing out on his forehead like opaque pearls, and for the time being he forgot the 'frillies reserved for special occasions'.

As for the man who could have answered poor Sergeant-Major Bull's question, he was sleeping the sleep of the just. Lying in his bunk, snoring gently, Sergeant Schulze was at peace with the world, his mind full of Mrs Sergeant-Major Bulle and her loving nature, in particular that hairy beaver of hers. What the morrow would bring did not trouble 'Frau Schulze's handsome son', as the big NCO was wont to describe himself, one bit. He slept on totally unconcerned with the horrors to come . . .

BOOK TWO

The Pimple and the Tiger

One

The winter was almost there. Though it might mean further hardships for hard-pressed citizens of Leningrad, it also gave them new hope. 'General Frost' would now take over and protect them from the Fritzes. For the Germans would not attack under the terrible conditions and sub-zero temperatures that would prevail once the winter had started to bite.

Of course, the exhausted civilians, living off starvation rations, still fell dead on the Neva Prospekt. There they would lie, ignored by their follow citizens, too numb to care, until the soldiers came to heave them into their trucks like logs of wood. If they were lucky, the 'stiffs' would be transported away before the cannibals crept out at night to carve off the soft human meat of the inner thighs or the rump.

The city was still completely surrounded save for what the citizens called the 'Lake of Life'. This was the ice road across the Lake of Ladoga, maintained at all costs twenty-four hours a day. Here the supplies which kept the besieged city going were driven across, usually at night, with the ice groaning and sighing under the weight of the trucks and occasionally cracking, leaving the vehicles to disappear through the great fissures in the broken ice. But still now with the German pressure eased, they kept on coming, bringing in food and new troops to be sent to the perimeter of the defences.

Hourly they poured into Lengingrad, marching ten abreast, singing lustily past the Bourse, the Winter Palace along the River Neva, giving a feeling of security and hope to the old crones trundling their dead on sledges to the mass graves or holes in the ice over the river into which they could plunge burdens which had become too heavy for their frail bodies.

Some of the older people regained enough confidence in the future to slip cautiously into the Kazan Cathedral and chant their prayers, standing up and directed by bearded priests, who, frightened as they were of communist repression, knew that they had the support of the ordinary citizens once more. Among themselves they whispered, 'Communism is dead; Christianity is alive again,' and hoped that once the great siege was lifted, they would be allowed their freedom to do what they liked once more, no longer dominated by the Godless *apparatchiks* of the communist regime.

But the Fritzes were still there, despite the hopes of the long-suffering citizens. Long-range German guns, some of them used during the siege of Sevastpol, still shelled the Uritsky Square the area of the Griboydevoy Canal. At night German reconnaissance planes continued to fly over the city, dropping their 'Christmas Trees', great bundles of flares which turned night into day; and the German propaganda companies would broadcast their boasts and threatening messages to the men in the frontline, promising them pardons and safe conducts if they came over to the Fritzes now before it was too late.

But those who knew of these things, and the Soviet authorities saw to it that only a few of them did, were no longer frightened and impressed. They told each other, their eyes bulging feverishly out of their skin-tight, emaciated faces, 'Once the Fritzes are driven back a few kilometres the artillery bombardments will cease . . . The food convoys will get through once more and there'll be vodka, bread and sausages in plenty for us all, not just for the big shots.'

And even the 'big shots' – who encouraged the pathetic hopes of these skeletal wretches, living for their dreams though they might well be dead of starvation before the day was out – believed the rumours, too, in part. The Fritzes had taken a pounding and surely they had no hope of mounting a winter offensive with 'General Frost' about to snap into action on the Red Army's side?

The Red Army commanders who had been consistently defeated by the Fritzes virtually ever since Germany had invaded Russia were not so sanguine. They knew the Germans' virtues as soldiers and their strengths. They felt the citizens of Leningrad were expecting the impossible. Now that winter was almost here, their talk was almost exclusively of the great link-up between the forces in the city and the Red Army on the Volkhov Front to the south of Leningrad.

Facing the city's political leaders, they would offer praise, but then lecture them with, 'Comrades, you and your people have had a very rough time this last year. We understand that, don't we, comrades?' The heavy-set men in the uniform of the Red Army, their breath smelling of the vodka which was the only thing that seemed to keep them going, would nod their agreement. 'But we of the Leningrad Front and our comrades of the Volkhov Front can't produce miracles out of a hat, you must realise, we just don't have the men and the supplies.'

The city's political leaders (most of them former factory workers, who had joined the Party early and carved their way ruthlessly to the top) knew they had to prove to their 'people', the citizens of Leningrad, that they had their best interests at heart; and there was only one way to do that. That was to get the military to attack and raise the long, murderous siege by linking up.

They'd say, almost like a religious creed, 'We realize that, comrades, but you must understand our position too. Hundreds die every day and there are those here in Leningrad who maintain that the comrades in the Kremlin and the *Stavka*[*] have deliberately made little attempt to relieve us because they don't like us Leningraders.'

Always when the Kremlin was brought up, the Red Army officers would lower their gaze like schoolboys caught with their hands in the apple barrel. Everyone knew that 'Old Leather Face', as they called the pock-marked Soviet dictator Stalin behind his back, had his spies everywhere. None of them wanted to end up in the gulag, or worse, against a wall with the firing squad pointing their rifles at them.

[*] Russian General Staff.

The political leaders, who knew that their own fates would be sealed if Leningrad fell to the Fritzes, would press home their advantage, knowing that they had little to lose. 'With General Frost already on the march, comrade officers, it should not be too difficult to throw back the Fritzes and force the link-up. How many more of our people, I ask you, comrades, must die miserably before that objective is achieved?' The habitual plea from the commissars would often be too much for the military. They were hard men. They had no time for emotion. Emotions belonged to silly old *babushkas*, who still believed in God and religion.

Often they would halt the proceedings and allow the civilians a little treat in order to take the tension off the conference. An orderly would appear, carrying a great steaming samovar of red-hot real tea. 'The tea is genuine,' they would boast, 'came across the Lake last night.' Hurriedly the orderly would ladle a small portion of strawberry jam into the cups as a sweetener – most of them, soldier and civilian alike, had not tasted sugar for months, perhaps years – and then pour the hot tea after it. Sometimes there would even be vodka.

But as the winter drew ever closer and with it the knowledge, as far as the civilian commissars were concerned, that General Frost was on his way to defeat the Fritzes, the civilians grew bolder. Their demands for a link-up attack became ever more urgent and could not be appeased with cups of tea and vodka.

They started to tell the officers what they should do to prepare for the great, long-awaited link-up. 'We call it the "Pimple",' they would say. 'It is the only high ground on the whole Leningrad Front. We know you soldiers call it Height 560, but for us in Leningrad it has always been the "Pimple".'

The officers would nod, dreading what was to come. For they knew more about the 'Pimple' than these native-born Leningraders. They knew, too, what the cost of taking that damned height, which would dominate their flanks below in any attack, might be. Still they listened a little helplessly.

'To break the Fritz stranglehold on the city, comrade officers,' they would preach fervently, 'you need to capture that "Pimple". Once it is taken, you dominate the enemy's front and then the link-up can be organized without any great losses on the part of our brave boys.'

In vain the officers tried to explain they had already lost a couple of battalions of 'our brave boys', perhaps some two thousand men, trying to capture the height in the previous year.

But the civilians would object, 'Yes, but that was last year when the weather favoured the Fritzes with their tanks and heavy guns. Now with General Frost on his way, the weather favours us, comrade officers.'

Afterwards the officers would hold their heads as if in despair, drinking their daily rations of a hundred grams of vodka in one go, moaning, 'If anyone mentions that shitting General Frost to me again, I'll shoot myself, I swear I will.'

But as hope grew in the city, with the battered streets glistening with hoar frost in the morning now and the bodies in the gutters frozen solid, so that they no longer swelled with gas and burst their guts as they had done previously, the question of the 'Pimple' grew so big that the staff officers could no longer appease the civilian commissars' demands for action.

As November 1942 began to give way to a freezingly cold December, the staff knew that their commander, the General himself, would have to make a decision: should they risk attacking the height that dominated the whole of Leningrad and chance staggering losses that might delay the great link-up even longer; should they give way to the demands of the civilians and take that overwhelming risk?

Thus it was that while in faraway Germany, the Vulture prepared his troopers for the unknown battle for Leningrad to come, General Govorov, the commander of the Leningrad Front, faced up to the senior civilian commissar, Zhdanov. Zhdanov, big, balding, brash, thought this winter's day with the snow falling steadily outside the general's HQ, that he had the army commander on the run. Even he could not deny that the winter was here; General Frost had arrived and he was a new ally to be reckoned with. He was not prepared to pull his punches. The soldier began with the usual litany of apologies, 'We're doing our best, comrade . . . We understand your problems, but you must understand—'

'*Boshe moi*!' he swore angrily. 'That is bullshit, Comrade General. What you don't understand is that my people *demand* an end to this misery of the siege. It's been going on for too long.' His eyes blazed with fury and suddenly the general felt naked and somewhat ashamed under that glare. 'What if my people simply give up? Won't tolerate the siege any longer, take power into their own hands and surrender the place to the Fritzes, eh? How would that look in Moscow, comrade. The Leningraders handing over their city to the Fritzes on a silver platter.'

The general looked at the commissar aghast. 'Why . . .' he stuttered, 'you must not even think such dastardly things, comrade . . . It's high treason . . . The people of Leningrad will hold out a little longer. They *must*!'

Zhdanov laughed scornfully. '*Must?* What are you talking about, Comrade General? You go and tell my people that when at this very moment they are cooking the paste from the back of the wallpaper and boiling down old leather boots to get some kind of nourishment to keep them alive for another day . . . and only a couple of kilometres away, the fat Fritz bastards are stuffing themselves with fried potatoes and sausage and swilling their muck down with schnaps and beer. *You* –' he pointed a dirty, tobacco-stained forefinger accusingly at the general so that the latter staggered back a pace or two in alarm – 'go and tell people to hold out!'

Govorov recovered himself a little. He patted the sweat away from his forehead with an immaculate white linen handkerchief, realizing that he was facing a very serious crisis. The people of Leningrad had long been known for their independence. The descendants of those who had helped Peter the Great* to build the city which had originally been named after him had always been single-minded and independent, believing themselves superior to the Moscovites. The general knew they were quite capable of taking matters into their own hands if provoked enough and trying to come to some kind of a deal with the Fritzes. The very thought of such an eventuality sent

* Leningrad was called originally Petrograd, 'Peter's City'. *Transl.*

his head reeling; it probably would coat him not only his command but his life, too.

The general swallowed hard. 'All right then, Comrade Commissar,' he said. 'You shall have your first attack.'

The civilian's face lit up. 'The Pimple?'

'Yes, the Pimple.'

'How?'

'A surprise attack in battalion strength. Just a slight artillery bombardment to both sides of the height to keep the Fritzes there in their trenches. Then up and at them in a *coup de main*. There'll be severe losses –' the general shrugged carelessly – 'but that won't matter as long as we take the objective.'

Zhdanov beamed. 'Thank you, General.' He held out his hand. The general took it. It was soft and damp. It was a Party official's hand, one that had never seen any really hard work for years; one that was occupied behind a desk, signing orders that would send other men to their deaths. '*Davoi, Tovarisch*.'

'*Davoi*.'

Five minutes later the Party boss had gone, still beaming, a stiff water glass full of pepper vodka down his threat, so that he could brave the snowstorm now raging outside. Behind him, General Govorov stared at the falling snow, his mind still in a turmoil. He knew from past experience he couldn't take the Pimple with a single battalion. A whole division would be needed to take that damned height and he hadn't a division of infantry to spare. All the same he could not face up to the alternative. He had to be seen by the damned Party bosses and civilians as doing something.

Then he had it. He picked up the intercom phone which connected him with his chief-of-staff. 'Pavlov,' he snapped, 'alert Penal Battalion 555. I want them readied for an immediate attack.'

'But Comrade General, half of them still haven't rifles. They'll be slaughtered.'

The general laughed scornfully. 'What does that matter? Let those traitors, Jews and gulag rats be slaughtered. They can go down as heroes who died *failing* to take the Pimple.' He slammed down the phone, suddenly pleased with himself . . .

Two

Dawn came reluctantly. In their dugouts, the men of the Penal Battalion squatted on the frozen straw, shivered and scratched the lice which covered their emaciated bodies. Those who had rifles hung on to them grimly in the hope they might be able to use them and save their miserable lives in what was to come. Those who hadn't wondered what they could do to survive.

Behind them at the base of the slope, the NKVD troops in their green caps were beginning to form up. The well-fed troops of the Secret Police were all armed with round-barrelled tommy guns; and they weren't intended for use on the Fritzes somewhere above at the top of the 'Pimple'. They were to be turned on any one of the Penal Battalion who refused to get out of his dugout and attack, or turned and attempted to run when it started.

Now the barrage was coming to an end and in the German lines the red flares were beginning to sail into the winter sky indicating that help was needed or reinforcements to make up for casualties suffered during the artillery bombardment. The flares meant, too, that the Fritzes knew they were coming and they'd be ready for the Penal Battalion's assault.

Dawn. A chill wind blew across the snowy hillside. Reluctantly the officers blew their whistles. Equally reluctantly the ex-prisoners rose from their trenches, like grey ghosts rising from their graves. In the skeletal trees the birds flapped their wings, angry at being disturbed. Cawing hoarsely, they ascended into the snow-filled sky. Nobody spoke. They no longer even trembled in the bone-chilling cold or attempted to stamp their feet or swing their arms in order to restore some warmth to their skinny bodies.

Their officers, convicted men like themselves, took their places in front of the trenches. They, at least, were armed. Whistles shrilled. Down below, out of range, a brass band swung into a brisk military march to encourage these doomed men. '*Davoi*!' the officers cried, their breath fogging grey in the cold. They swung their free arms forward and yelled, '*Slava Krasnaya Armya*!' Weakly the men replied, 'Long Live the Red Army,' and then they were moving upwards through the flying snowflakes, with the NKVD behind them, their tommy guns aimed at the attackers' backs.

Steadily they progressed up the Pimple. The only sound was the hiss of the snowstorm and their own harsh, hectic breathing. Up above them, clouded by the flying snow, the Germans in their positions remained obstinately still as if taunting them to come ever closer and be slaughtered. But every now and again a flare exploded above their heads, colouring their skull-like faces in a garish, unnatural light. Still they marched on to their deaths, cherishing the hope, as all men will, that it would be the others who would die, not they.

'Steady,' their officers urged at intervals. Behind them, the NKVD men used harsher terms. 'Move your stinking gulag arses, you scum,' they called and made threatening gestures with the tommy guns. 'Do you want to live for ever, you dogs?' And they were too worn and brow-beaten even to snarl a reply.

The height seemed endlessly long. Now they were panting. Some were even wet with a sweat of apprehension as they came on and on. A few prayed but not many.

At their head, his uniform covered in snow, the battalion commander drew his sabre. He was still a proud and patriotic Russian soldier despite everything that had happened to him since his battalion had run away in the summer of 1941 and he had been cashiered and sent to the gulag. He placed the sabre over his shoulder momentarily then he swung it over his fur-capped head with a bold flourish. Ignoring the crack and hiss of the flares exploding everywhere now, he cried at the top of his voice, '*Battalion* . . . battalion will charge. *Urrah!*'

'*Urrah!*' Even the deserters and petty crooks took up the old Russian cry, which had put the fear of death into the Germans so many times in the past.

They swept forward in the same instant that one single shot rang out. The battalion commander staggered. The fur cap slipped foolishly down his face. His sword slipped from suddenly nerveless fingers and he fell. Then they were springing over his dying body as the German machine guns opened up and the slaughter commenced.

Carried away by the wild, unreasoning bloodlust of battle, the criminals of the penal battalion sprang over the writhing bodies of their comrades, screaming and shrieking fervently with rage and frustration, to be hit and felled the very next moment. Still they came on, knowing that if they broke and ran back, the tommy-gunners of the NKVD would be waiting for them.

Up on the height, the German machine-gunners twisted their 'Hitler saws', as they nicknamed their Spandau machine guns, from left to right mercilessly. Great gaps appeared in the ranks of the Russians advancing up the slope through the driving snow. It was a virtual white-out, but at that range, the gunners couldn't miss. Now the advancing men had ceased to shout their battle cry. The spirit was dying quickly. But there was no escape for them. They were fated to die one way or another and with typical Russian fatalism they accepted the fact. They died by their scores and in the end by their hundreds. So that only a handful reached the German perimeter to be shot down by officers and NCOs waiting for them there, taking aim with one hand behind their backs, as if they were on some peacetime range, firing at wooden and canvas targets.

Within the hour it was virtually all over. The NKVD captain reported to his senior. The latter reported to the chief-of-staff of the Leningrad Front. He called Zhdanov and reported to the senior civilian commissar, his voice full of mock sorrow, 'I am sad to inform you, comrade, that the attack on the Pimple has been a failure. We have lost a whole battalion in the attempt. The brave fellows went to their deaths, knowing the vital importance of their objective. Unfortunately—' he broke off as if he were too overcome by sorrow to continue.

Sitting at his desk behind the chief-of-staff, General Govorov lit another *paperoki* and puffed out the smoke like a man content with himself. 'Useless mouths to feed actually, Pavlov,' he commented. 'Now those damned civilians will perhaps let us get on with our work as soldiers without interfering.' He nodded at the bottle of pepper vodka. The chief-of-staff understood. He poured a water glass full for his superior and then a smaller one for himself.

The general raised his glass as if in toast. '*Naszoroya*,' he cried.

The chief-of-staff repeated the toast. It was almost as if they were celebrating a victory . . .

'*Grossartig*!' Hitler stamped his jackbooted right foot down hard and Blondi, his Alsatian bitch, alarmed by the sudden noise fled into the corner of the briefing room. Hitler and his military advisers didn't notice. They were too excited by the great news from the Leningrad front.

Field Marshal Keitel, tall, wooden-faced and stiff-backed, naturally agreed with Hitler; he always did. 'Yes, *mein Führer*,' he said, 'we haven't had such good news from the East for a long time – all this damned winter in fact. It means—'

'Means that my plan is correct,' Hitler beat him to it. 'A single company of ordinary German infantry beats off an attack by a whole Russian battalion and wipes the Ivans out with just a handful of casualties of their own. It is clear that the Russians have no longer the stomach for a real fight at Leningrad that they once had. It strengthens my determination to go ahead with the surprise attack this winter, rotten weather or not, and finally clear up that mess at Leningrad.'

General Gehlen, standing in the second row of the generals crowded around the sand table of the northern front, cleared his throat noisely. But for the time being, Hitler was paying no heed to his chief of Intelligence in the East. Gehlen's sallow face flushed, but he contained his temper. He had long learned to do that in the Führer's presence. He'd bide his time and then set these pompous, hidebound fools to rights.

'If the Russians can't take the key Height –' he clicked his fingers impatiently.

'560,' Keitel supplied the figure immediately. He was good at such things.

'Yes, 560, which dominates their two fronts around Leningrad and their key objectives, Schusselberg – there – and Sinyavino – over there – then we can be sure that the calibre of their troops in and around Leningrad is poor. So, despite the fact that winter is on their side, in the main, our men will still be able to achieve victory.'

Gehlen saw his chance. As Hitler paused for breath and Blondi came from her hiding place to nestle near her master's boot once more, he said, 'In regard to the calibre of the enemy troops, *mein Führer* –'

The front rank brass – Keitel, Jodl, Admiral Dönitz and the rest – turned to stare at this low-ranking general who had dared to break into the Leader's exposition. Gehlen continued hastily with, 'Yesterday my people went over the ground where the attack failed, gentlemen. We came to a certain conclusion about the calibre of the enemy troops who attacked.'

Field Marshal Keitel was about to stop Gehlen, but Hitler raised his hand for silence and Gehlen went on. 'We did a count of the number and type of weapon the Russians carried. We discovered that only half of them had been armed and the whole battalion had attacked without a single machine gun.'

There was an angry murmur in the room and Blondi thought it wiser to cock her leg and urinate against her master's boot before disappearing into the safety of the corner once more. Strangely enough Hitler didn't explode as he often did on such occasions. Instead he said, 'Pray continue, Herr Gehlen. How do you explain this?'

'Very easily, sir. The attackers weren't regular infantry. They belonged to a penal battalion. Under normal circumstances it would be their job to clear mines and the like by simply walking into the minefield and exploding them with their own feet.

In other words, they weren't fighting troops, but simply cannonfodder.'

Hitler took the information very calmly, unlike his staff who looked both puzzled and grave. 'A penal battalion, eh? Well, my dear Gehlen, one can interpret intelligence in more than one way, as you know. Perhaps that means they are running out of regular infantry.' He dismissed the matter with a casual wave of his hand. 'The plan will work,' he said confidently, 'once we get Wotan in position. And why will it work?' He answered his own question with the kind of bravado he had exhibited back in '39–40 when everything had gone the way he wanted it and he had achieved victory after victory so that it seemed that nothing was ever going to stop him. 'In one word. Because of the Tiger.'

Some of his listeners, including Gehlen, looked blank, for he had never interested himself in technical matters; he had left that area to the junior members of the Foreign Armies East's staff.

Hitler saw the look. He laughed and added, 'The Tiger is the most powerful tank in the world. Sixty tons of Krupp steel, which cannot be penetrated by any gun currently in production. The Soviet T-34' – he meant the Russians' most powerful tank – 'is puny in comparison. A Tiger handled by a skilled crew and in the most favourable position could probably knock out a whole brigade of Russian T-34s.' His smile broadened. 'No, gentlemen, once the Wotan is in position and has received the new armoured monster on wheels, I think I can confidently say we shall be celebrating Christmas 1942 in Leningrad . . .'

Three

The pace that the Vulture had set for the men of Wotan was tremendous. From 'reveille' at five thirty in the morning to 'lights out' at nine thirty, both the old hares and the greenbeaks were kept moving mercilessly. Their breakfast, a bowl of weak pea soup, a hunk of black bread and sugarless ersatz coffee made of acorns, was the only time the men had to sit down. For a quarter of an hour exactly. Then the Vulture would come striding into the mess halls, followed by the Bull and the orderly officer, slashing at the tables with his riding crop, so that the plates and mess tins rattled, crying, '*Los Ihre Hunde* . . . come on, you dogs, are you going to sit there for ever?'

Thereafter the men were running or marching for hours on end, bullied and chivvied by the Bull and NCOs of his ilk, watched all the time by an angry-faced Vulture, who seemed to be here, there and everywhere, slapping the greenbeaks across the face when they didn't meet up to his standards, fixing his baleful gaze on the panting old hares and threatening them with the dreaded military prison at Torgau if they didn't get 'the lead out of your lazy arses'.

Behind his back, the men would mutter and threaten, the old hares promising they'd 'do the bastard in' once they went back to the front – 'a nice fat slug in the small of his nasty back'. But if the Vulture heard the mumbled threats and dire predictions, he paid no heed to them. Relentlessly, never seeming to tire, he pursued his cruel back-breaking routine, as if every minute was precious.

Every morning after the meagre breakfast, the anti-tank-gunners would take their gun 'for a walk', pushing and pulling the heavy cannon up hills and down steep valleys, their faces brick-red, gasping like old men in the throes of a final attack of asthma. Meanwhile the young panzer grenadiers would be given shovels and told to dig themselves in. This they would do as slowly as they dared, glad of the rest. Not for long. Suddenly there would be the roar of tank engines and the startled and abruptly very frightened greenbeaks would be aware of the four or five Mark III tanks bearing down upon them and realize why they had been ordered to dig the holes. Minutes later the Mark IIIs would come crawling over their holes, where they crouched in absolute panic, filling their lungs with the stink of fuel, churning the edges of the crumbling soil as if threatening to bury them alive before departing, leaving them crying, with trousers soaked with their own urine – and sometimes worse – and a mocking Bull shouting, 'What kind of frigging soldiers are you lot, pissing yer pants like that?'

Kuno von Dodenburg, despite his illness, was able to keep up with the tremendous pace set by the Vulture relatively easily (after all, he was a regular) and in essence he approved of this strict training. The men, especially the greenbeaks, would need all the stamina they could muster if they were to fight in the Russian winter. All the same he didn't agree with the way the Vulture went about it. As he said to Dietz, during a break in the training when a soldier who had been run over by a tank had had to have his leg amputated to free him from beneath the tank's tracks, 'The men must become hard, but we want thinking soldiers too, not a bunch of automatons, who go to their deaths not even knowing the reason why.'

Dietz nodded his head but said nothing, gritting his teeth as the battalion doctor started to cut through the youth's leg bones with his saw and the poor kid started to scream his head off. For the Vulture had forbiden the MO to give him anything to relieve the pain, telling the white-faced spectators, 'You'll see what it's like to be hurt in Russia, where there are no facilities. There'll you learn to stand up to pain all right.'

But if Dietz and most of the battalion's officers and men wouldn't, or dared not, complain, naturally Sergeant Schulze did (though even he dared not open his mouth in the Vulture's presence). 'Shitting awful fodder,' he moaned to Matz as they hid in the officers' latrines and enjoyed a furtive smoke. 'Why, all day yesterday I never ate no more than a tin of Old Man.' He meant tinned Italian meat reputedly made from the corpses of old men who had died in the workhouse. 'No suds even at a weekend.' He shook his big head miserably. 'If it wasn't for the bit o' four-legged beast with Hannalore now and agen, I just don't know how I'd keep going . . . and on that kind of fodder, I can't keep servicing her much longer, I'm that weak. Wasting away. I only did it three times last week. I honestly swear, Matzi, old house, I'm going impotent.' For a moment his eyes seemed to his old running mate to flood with tears of self-pity.

'Tut, tut,' Matz said in mock sympathy and then both of them heard the well-remembered stamp of heavy boots, which could mean only one thing. Sergeant-Major Bulle was on the prowl, on the Vulture's orders, looking for people like themselves who were dodging the gruelling routine that the CO had set for SS Assault Battalion Wotan. Hastily they doused their cigarettes and crept out of the rear exit, not before Schulze, however, had dropped his cigarette end in the Vulture's own private thunderbox: something he knew would anger the beak-nosed commander beyond measure.

But the two old hares were wrong if they thought that the Bull was solely preoccupied with carrying out the Vulture's orders. In fact the big brute of a sergeant-major had other and more personal matters on his mind. It was who was slipping his wife Hannelore 'a fly link', as he would have put it in his own words. For he was sure now, despite the pressure of the Vulture's training programme, that someone had energy enough and the time to dance the 'mattress polka' with his wife. But who and how? Why else would Hannelore refuse what he had to offer her: a piece of salami that had been fondled and admired in whorehouses from Norway to North Africa?

But who was the swine who was dicking her when he was on duty, serving Folk, Fatherland and Führer? A man like that should be shot for treachery to the holy cause of National

Socialist Germany. At all events, if he caught the sneaking bastard he'd tie a loop in his cock in zero comma seconds.

He sniffed suddenly, his train of thought broken. 'Lung torpedoes' – good quality 'lung torpedoes', here in the officers' shitehouse. He progressed further down the corridor until he came to a stop outside a stall with a large notice adorning it proclaiming that this was 'The Private Sanitary Facility of the Commanding Officer. SS Assault Regiment Wotan.' He gasped with shock. A cigarette end, already wet and beginning to shred tobacco, was floating there, blatantly mocking the sanctity of the place. 'Holy strawsack!' The Bull exploded at the sight. Who had dared to do such a thing? The way that the Vulture ensured the sanctity of his own private thunderbox could make something like this a hanging offence. For a moment or two, he was so shocked that he couldn't think clearly. Finally he realized he had to do something before the Vulture came for his pre-luncheon piss. There'd be all hell to pay if he discovered the cigarette end lying there, staring up at him, clear evidence that his authority as the CO of the Waffen SS's premier regiment was being challenged; and who would he vent his rage upon? 'Naturally me,' the Bull said aloud, already mentally cringing at the tongue-lashing the Vulture would inflict upon him. But could he pick up the offending lung torpedoes? It went against the grain. After all he was the regiment's senior NCO.

It was just then that he caught sight of the little *Hiwi*, Igor, passing, carrying a bucket over his brawny arm. What he was up to and where he was going, though it seemed to be in the general direction of the senior NCOs' quarters, the Bull didn't know. But that didn't matter. The Mongolian sub-human had come just in time. 'Hey, you Popov,' the Bull called. 'Over here at the double, arse-with-ears.'

Igor turned and hesitated.

'You heard me,' the Bull exclaimed, a little angrily, 'or have yer been eating big beans? At the double, I said.'

'No big beans,' Igor replied in his worse German. 'Job for lady sergeant. In a hurry.'

'Then pick up them fag ends and get on with yer business. *Nun wirds bald?*'

Obligingly, Igor picked the cigarette ends from the water and placed them in his bucket. And then he was off on his errand, whatever it was. It was only after he had disappeared into the entrance of the senior NCOs' quarters that the Bull recalled the Popov sub-human had said something about a 'lady sergeant'. He cleared his throat noisily and said to himself, 'Hannelore's a lady sergeant for him.' He frowned. Despite what her old man had said before he'd married Hannalore, she'd been no pure-white virgin. But would she let one of those Russian apes get his dirty paws up her knickers? He knew in wartime everything was possible; women would sink to any depth to get the other. But with a Popov sub-human? He was still pondering this overwhelming question when the First Company clerk came out of the company orderly room, waving a message. 'Urgent message for Company Commander von Dodenburg, Sergeant-Major. Can I go and deliver it, sir?'

The Bull nodded absently, 'Yes, off yer go and tie up the top button of the tunic, first. We're Wotan remember, not a sloppy bunch of shit-shovellers from the *Wehrmacht*.'

That night Kuno von Dodenburg was on the train, beginning the long journey to the tank training ground in remotest Bavaria at Grafenwöhr, wondering why he had been summoned there so surprisingly, but guessing at the same time that it had something to do with what was being planned for SS Assault Regiment Wotan. Behind him, he'd left an almost exhausted regiment, filled with men who bore mutiny in their hearts, and that mutiny was directed at one man solely, Colonel Geier, known as the Vulture.

But that night as von Dodenburg had set off on his long journey southwards and silence had finally fallen on Wotan's barracks, the worn-out troopers already long sunk into an exhausted sleep in their wooden bunks, the first of the trucks began to arrive. The guard commander and the sentries had already been alerted to let the trucks through without any kind of a check; and the Vulture himself was personally present at the great gate to the barracks to ensure that his orders were carred out.

One by one, they rolled through the open gate and headed for the gym, which had been sealed off at the Vulture's instructions, leaving behind them, as that night's guard commander, Sergeant Schulze, explained in puzzlement to Corporal Matz the following morning, 'a kind of stink of carbolic as if they was some kind of laundry unit. Funny that, can't explain it mesen.'

But that was why the Vulture had been ordered to accept these sealed-off trucks after 'lights out' and with only a handful of most necessary personnel on duty to see them. Hurriedly, again supervised by the Vulture, the men from Foreign Armies East started to unload their bundles and stow them towards the end of the gym, where they were covered by great tarpaulins which the men of the Intelligence unit had also brought with them. But not before Igor, the *Hiwi*, prowling the SS barracks as always, noting everything with his seemingly innocent peasant gaze, had spotted the contents of the bundles.

Within an hour the delivery was completed and the trucks were speeding away, leaving Schulze, who watched them go (taking furtive nips from his flatman and wishing he was getting up Hannelore's drawers at this moment, and not listening to the snores of the off-duty men), no wiser. Settled in the potato cellar which was his home, Igor too puzzled about those mysterious bundles. More than once, lying on the potatoes, trying to keep warm – and failing – he asked himself why should the SS, recipent of the best equipment in the German Army, make such a fuss of a delivery of old faded *Wehrmacht* uniforms?

Four

A staff car was waiting for Kuno von Dodenburg as the train halted at the little station of Grafenwöhr to let off a draft of black-uniformed young tank crews obviously being sent to this remote Bavarian place, already deep in the annual winter snow, for training. The driver, a corporal in the SS, though his sleeve bore no indication of what SS unit he belonged to,* saluted smartly and said, 'You are to eat breakfast first, sir, after your journey and then you are to report to the unit commander at nine hundred hours, sir.'

'What unit, Corporal?' Kuno asked, and shivered in the sudden icy cold after the warm fug of the troop train.

The driver didn't seem to hear. Instead, he picked up Kuno's bag and pack and carried them to the big pre-war Horch. He drove off, leaving the happy tank corps recruits laughing and snowballing each other like the schoolkids they really were. Sitting in the comfortable seat, as the snow-capped mountains started to slide by, Kuno envied them a little their carefree approach to soldiering and then he concentrated on the mystery of this sudden summons to the great tank training ground. His orders stated simply that he was to report to Grafenwöhr, but there was no mention of to which particular unit and for what purpose. It was all a bit confusing, but then, old hare that he was, Kuno von Dodenburg told himself that he'd soon find out what the drill was and, if he knew the Waffen SS, it'd probably turn out to be something unpleasant.

Fifteen minutes later, when he could already hear the twang and thud of tank cannon being fired on the other side of the

* SS units bore the title of their unit on their lower right sleeve.

mountain range, indicating that they were getting closer to the training grounds, the corporal hit his brakes abruptly. The big Horch shimmied and skidded and for a moment Kuno thought they had hit a patch of ice concealed beneath the new snowfall. He opened his mouth to curse the driver and tell him to keep a closer eye on the surface of the read when the curse died on his lips.

It wasn't ice which had occasioned the red-faced driver to brake so suddenly. It was something else, crashing through the firs on the right side of the road, snapping them like matchsticks and churning up the snow into a furious white wake, as the monster slammed into the road, perhaps ten metres in front of the Horch.

'*Gross Gott*!' Kuno exclaimed, as a huge tank of a kind he had never seen before continued its massive progress across the road and went smashing into the firs on the other side and disappeared moments later, leaving behind it a trail of severed green fronds and broken trees. 'In three devils' name, what was that monster?'

But the flushed driver, busy restarting his engine, didn't seem to hear Kuno's question. For von Dodenburg the mystery deepened even more in the mess where he was served his breakfast of real bean coffee – something he hadn't drunk for many months – fresh rolls and as much of the rich Bavarian butter he could smear on them. Although the breakfast came as a pleasant surprise – there were even boiled eggs – it was his companions who helped to increase his mystification.

By German standards they were small men, though very weathered and tough looking, wearing a uniform he couldn't identify. All seemed to be carrying a small curved knife and all wore a small shoulder patch in what appeared to be their national colours with the word '*Suomi*' written on it. But what the word meant he couldn't decipher. A couple of times he attempted to speak to his neighbour. But all he received by way of a reply was a stiff bow from the waist before the officer handed him the butter or another roll, as if that was what Kuno had asked for.

An hour later the puzzled young officer was enlightened a

little when he was ushered into the office of a tall, one-armed colonel who wore the arm title of the *Leibstandarte*, the senior SS division, known as the 'Adolf Hitler Bodyguard'. The colonel was an imposing figure and, if his towering height and bearing were anything to go by, he had once been one of the original founding members of that elite formation. But he was friendly and, to judge by the missing arm and the silver wound medal, which indicated he had been wounded more than three times, he had seen his share of combat.

'All right, von Dodenburg,' he cut in, as Kuno started to introduce himself, 'enough. Park yourself on that chair over there. We all know who you are. With a bit of luck –' he touched his empty sleeve significantly – 'you'll be commanding your own regiment before you're thirty.' He gave Kuno a brief smile and then got down to business. 'Now, I'm going to tell you as much as I can, anyway as much as you need to get on with the job you've been landed with.'

Kuno nodded as if he understood, which he didn't. Outside, it was snowing very hard now. But the hiss of the heavy snowfall didn't quite drown the roar of a massive engine coming from somewhere and Kuno von Dodenburg guessed that engine belonged to the monster which had nearly crashed into the car on the way to the remote camp.

'A little history first. You know we pioneered tank warfare from '39 to '41. Then the Ivans came up with that T-34 of theirs. Caught us with our knickers right down about our ankles, I can tell you. Our Mark IV was no match for it and when the Ivans started building it in large numbers and throwing them at us in their hundreds some of our tank people got the message. Rather belatedly, I must admit. Cost me my flipper.' Again he touched his empty sleeve. 'But that's another story. Anyway, General der Panzertruppe Guderian got cracking. Together with Minister Speer, the head of the Ammunition and Armaments Ministry, he gave immediate priority to producing a tank which could outdo the T-34 and all other known enemy tanks and win the war for us.' He rose and, walking over to the little stand behind his desk, whipped the cloth away from its top to reveal the model of a low-slung tank, carrying what, in reality, would be a monstrous gun.

Kuno couldn't help it. He whistled in admiration. It was a model of the same tank that had come crashing out of the forest so surprisingly.

The colonel smiled. 'Yes, you might well whistle, von Dodenburg. That's the war-winner, all sixty tons of her with an 88mm cannon. It's the I-E, which one day you'll know as the Tiger . . .'

Over the next forty-eight hours, instructed by a mixed bag of civilian engineers and tank corps officers from Grafenwöhr's training staff, Kuno got to know the I-E, or Tiger as the one-armed colonel had called it, pretty well. It had its defects; he soon learned that. It was relatively slow. It consumed far too much fuel and broke down easily, because, as the engineers explained, it had been developed too quickly, before they could iron out what they called 'all the wrinkles'.

But despite all its defects, it was a very impressive fighting vehicle. On his second day at Grafenwöhr, they gave him a demonstration of the Tiger's staying power under fire. A captured British Churchill tank fired at its front glacis plate at a range of a couple of hundred metres. The British armour-piercing shells bounced off the thick steel plating harmlessly like glowing ping-pong balls. It was the same when they tried another captured T-34 on the Tiger at a wider range. The Russian shells gouged great shining silver stars on the monster's armour, but still they didn't penetrate.

As Kuno, who guessed Wotan was going to receive the Tiger – why else would he be shown this top-secret fighting vehicle? – told himself, nothing on tracks was going to stop it. He was even more impressed by the Tiger's great over-hanging 88mm cannon.

It fired both high explosive and armour-piercing shells, both better and more effective than any he had seen since the war had begun. On the afternoon of his second day, when he had become almost deaf with the constant noise of the last thirty-six hours, he had been given a demonstration of the 88's firepower.

A series of captured enemy tanks were brought up and the gun tested on them at various ranges. Finally the latest captured Anglo-American tank, the thirty-ton Sherman, was driven to within three hundred metres of where the Tiger waited, its engine beating like the heavy heart of some primeval monster preparing to obliterate its unsuspecting prey. Up went the red warning flares. Whistles shrilled to clear the range and then the 88mm thudded into action.

There was a harsh, ripping sound like a piece of tough calico being torn apart. The Tiger shuddered on its bogies. A flash of white. The sound of steel striking steel. A red flash. A puff of grey smoke. Next instant the ten-ton turret of the Sherman sailed lazily into the air to drop with an earth-shuddering thud some ten or fifteen metres away. Even the engineers who had developed the model and know its capabilities cried with delight and applauded that performance.

On the evening of the third day at Grafenwöhr, the mysterious one-armed colonel of the *Leibstandarte* called Kuno back to his office and handing him a generous whisky, 'captured from the Tommies at Dieppe'. He sat him down and, for some reason that von Dodenburg couldn't fathom, locked the door.

For a few moments the two of them sat there sipping the splendid whisky, while outside the wind howled in the dense fir forest and the snowflakes pelted against the blacked-out windows. Finally the colonel put his glass down and said, 'You're to get six of them – all we can spare.'

'You mean the Tigers?'

'Yes, one final check and they'll be on their way to Wotan. By night. We must keep the Tiger secret as long as possible.'

'But sir,' Kuno objected, 'no one can keep a secret in Berlin. It's full of prying eyes and gossipy people. Try to get a sixty-ton Tiger through to Wotan's barracks and half the capital would know the secret by the end of the day.'

The colonel gave him an amused smile. 'But they're not going to Berlin, von Dodenburg.'

'But sir, you said—'

'I know I did, von Dodenburg, but you won't be in Berlin when you receive your Tigers.'

'But where will we be, sir?' von Dodenburg asked a little helplessly.

'I'm afraid that must remain a secret until the powers that be see fit to tell you where.' The one-armed colonel pulled a face, as if he was fighting some inner conflict. At that moment, it seemed to Kuno that he was tempted to say more than he was allowed to. But after a moment it was clear that duty had won that brief battle, for the colonel added, voice subdued, as if he feared that someone might be outside in the raging snowstorm listening to them, ear pressed to the door. 'But I'll tell you this, I am sure you will meet those Finnish officers again soon. Now, you'd better get some shut-eye, von Dodenburg. You're catching the early morning train for Munich and then to Berlin.' He stretched out his one hand in that strange way that people who have had an arm amputated do. He pressed Kuno's hand hard, saying, '*Hals und Beinbruch*'.*

Then Kuno was outside in that raging storm, feeling more puzzled than ever.

* Literally: 'break your neck and leg', i.e. happy landings. *Transl.*

Five

'*Morgen, Soldaten*!' the Vulture cried, as he stood before the parade of SS Assault Regiment Wotan.

'*Morgen, Obersturmbannführer*!' the traditional morning greeting came back from nearly a thousand young voices. But there was no enthusiasm in them. The men were too worn, too angry, too resentful at their treatment at the hands of the Vulture over these last days. Geier had worked them into the ground and they hated it – and him.

The Vulture took his time. He knew how much they hated him. But that didn't matter. Hate was a stronger emotion than love; hate made for angry soldiers who would kill gladly to rid themselves of their frustrations. He eyed them through his monocle coldly, slapping his riding crop against the side of his highly polished riding boot, which with his baggy breaches marked him as a former *Wehrmacht* officer who'd joined the SS for more speedy advancement.

Finally he spoke. 'Tonight we depart. I cannot tell you your destination. But we leave at midnight and, as you will find out, SS Assault Regiment Wotan will have vanished by then to be replaced by Infantry Regiment 675 of the Greater German *Wehrmacht*.'

That puzzled them, as the Vulture knew it would. But he was not going to enlighten them any further; one should not spoil simple soldiers. It was their task to do as they were told and not ask why. In the *Wehrmacht*, they had called it *Kadavergehorsamkeit* – the 'obedience of the cadaver'.

'Just let me say this, however, soldiers.' The Vulture raised his voice. 'Any one of you who imparts this information to a non-authorized person will face trial and probably death immediately. Let that be understood. *Klar Soldaten*?'

'*Klar, Obersturmbannführer*,' came back the subdued murmur of agreement.

Watching and listening from the window of his quarters, von Dodenburg, tired and dirty from the long journey from Bavaria, yawned and told himself that the men showed absolutely no enthusiasm for this new assignment and the strange transformation from the Wotan to an ordinary *Wehrmacht* infantry battalion, which he guessed was to conceal the departure of an elite SS unit for the Eastern Front. But why such measures were being taken – and the business of the six Grafenwöhr Tigers – was beyond him. He started to comb his cropped blond hair and continued to listen.

'Now, let me mention a personal matter to you, simple soldiers, men of the CO corps and officers.' He paused and gave them a slight smile but there was no answering warmth in his cold blue eyes. 'My present rank is that of *Obersturmbannführer*.'

Von Dodenburg frowned. What in three devils' name was the Vulture on about? Why should his current rank interest the men of Wotan? Geier soon enlightened him and them.

He continued with: 'But my father was a general and proudly wore the general's stars at the age of thirty. I hope to emulate my dear departed parent. Before this war is over. I promise you men that I, too, shall be a general. General Geier, yes, and do you know how I shall do it?' He paused and a disgusted von Dodenburg told himself, the man was mad. How dare the Vulture cheapen Germany's great cause to bring hope and renewal to a decadent Old Europe with such talk of his own personal aims and ambitions? His eyes fell of Dietz commanding the parade. His normal ruddy, healthy face had suddenly gone very pale and Kuno had a momentary impression that he might faint. But he recovered swiftly and Kuno wondered if the same thoughts were going through his mind as through his own. Dietz was a hardened campaigner, a real old hare and front swine, tough and hard-boiled. Yet he, too, had Germany's cause at heart. He believed also that Wotan and the SS in general were a new kind of Napoleonic Imperial Guard, which, if needs be, would fight to the very end as they had done at Waterloo for their country and their emperor, in this case the new Greater German Empire and Adolf Hitler. How could the Vulture talk like this then in front of these brave young German men, volunteers all?

Up in front of the parade, the Vulture toyed with his new Knight's Cross of the Iron Cross dangling from his scrawny throat, as if he wished to assure himself that it was still there. 'I do not want you to like me, soldiers,' he rasped. 'I don't care even if you don't respect me – discipline will take care of any open disrespect.'

In the second rank, Sergeant Schulze gave one of his long, not unmusical farts, celebrated throughout the SS NCO Corps. The Vulture didn't hear and the Bull glared. But Schulze didn't care. 'I'll frigging disrespect you before I'm finished,' he promised.

'All I ask of you, soldiers,' the Vulture continued, 'is that you obey my orders with unquestioning obedience.' His hard eyes swept their ranks once more. 'And may God help any one of you, soldier, NCO, officer, who fails to do so.' He clicked to attention and raised his grey-gloved hand to the peak of his rakishly tilted cap with the dreaded skull-and-crossbones badge gleaming like silver. '*Dismiss*!'

Soon after dark that December evening as the subdued soldiers of SS Wotan filed into the gym to change into the shoddy worn uniforms of the *Wehrmacht* and, outside, the blacked-out trucks lined up to take them to the waiting troop train, two diverse things happened, which at the time no one could explain logically.

Behind a locked door in the privacy of his quarters, Major Dietz, the second-in-command, shot himself with his service pistol without leaving the usual explanatory suicide note behind; and Igor, the *Hiwi*, disappeared, never to be seen in Berlin again.

BOOK THREE

Journey to the Front

One

Midnight.

Despite the lateness of the hour, the station was still packed. Trains steamed in and out all the time, while under the shattered glass roof the loudspeakers boomed and re-boomed their announcements, directing them to all over the new German Empire. Paris . . . Brussels . . . Rome . . . Warsaw and a dozen more obscure cities and towns just behind the Russian front.

Women cried hysterically. Others sighed with heartfelt relief as they spotted a heavily laden loved one who had returned safely from fronts, which now stretched over three continents. There were even children waving swastika flags and skinny-legged Hitler Youths in their uniforms, shivering and rattling their cans to collect money for the 'Winter Relief'.

But there was no one to see off, wave and kiss and cry, as the shabby regiment of *Wehrmacht* infantry – cannonfodder written all over them – lined up, ready to board the troop train steaming at one of the dark, side platforms. Even the hard-eyed 'chained-up dogs', helmeted, with carbines slung over their broad shoulders, didn't so much as give them a passing glance. The infantry were too tame, too brow-beaten, it seemed to the military policemen, to attempt to desert.

The Bull, of course, was his usual officious, self-important self, though he looked distinctly shabby in the faded uniform of the an army sergeant-major. He stamped his boots and strode purposefully up and down the freezing platform, throwing threatening glances to left and right, as if he saw examples of ill-discipline on all sides. No one took any notice of his posturing; even the shivering greenbeaks were not impressed. As for the old hares, who had been this route before, they were too busy preparing for what was to come, already eyeing the best places on the long train, usually centred on the pot-bellied stove which each long compartment contained.

Most of them had already spent all the marks they possessed for comforts to last them for the days-long journey ahead. They knew that where they were going, marks would be worthless. As they quipped to each other, 'Have a short life and make a pretty corpse', to which Schulze in particular added his favourite saying for such occasions, 'Buy combs, lads, there's lousy times ahead.'

But the old hares had not spent their money on combs. Instead, they had laden themselves with rings of long-lasting salami bought from the furtive black-market dealers in the remoter parts of the great echoing station. Schnaps had come next, cheap firewater, which they had stowed in their flatmen, and even their water bottles, to wile away the boredom, together with the pornographic magazines and postcards, purchased from other dealers who peddled such items to troops heading for a front where the only kind of sexual relief would be what they called the 'five-fingered widow'. Though as Schulze, the expert, had reminded them, 'Better buy some Parisians, mates, just in case we stop in Warsaw. Yer knows what them Polack whores are like.'

Now, pushing in front of the miserable shivering greenbeaks, eyeing the places they had picked for themselves in the train, laden like pack mules, stinking of garlic sausage and cheap alcohol, they waited for permission to board under the stern gaze of the Vulture, who had managed to look as elegant as ever in his faded *Wehrmacht Oberstleutnant*'s uniform.

Puzzled as he was by what had happened at Grafenwöhr, the strange suicide of Major Dietz, which had come totally unexpectedly for him and this mysterious assignment on the Eastern Front, von Dodenburg still felt the old sensation of excitement and anticipation at the knowledge that he was going to the front once more. He knew, old hare that he was, he was being foolish. All the same, the thought of the danger, playing a kind of lethal roulette with his own young life, a slight frisson of fear, seemed to give him a heightened sense of awareness: the knowledge that a slight mistake on his part, a stroke of luck on the part of the enemy, and he could be a dead man in a matter of seconds. He knew those two old rogues over there, Schulze and Matz, drinking furtively from their flatmen, would have laughed at such thoughts: they were the born survivors. They would do their share, fight almost to the last, but in the end, they were no fatalists like Kuno supposed he was. If the '1,000 Year Empire', as the Führer called the new German empire, was fated not to survive the war, then perhaps he ought to go down with it. He grinned at his own gloomy thoughts and then wondered whether he had packed his lice powder; he'd need it where they were going.

Lice were also occupying Schulze's and Matz's thoughts and talk at that moment. In between slugs of their firewater, they lectured the awed greenbeaks on the kind of lice they would encounter on the Eastern Front. 'Felt lice,' they explained, 'as big as yer thumbnail most of the little buggers. They breed all the frigging time – nothing to do but sup yer blood and fuck. And –' Schulze raised a forefinger like a hairy pork sausage – 'they lay five frigging eggs a day. Think o' that. The eggs survive ten days, so, you greenbeaks, if yer don't do a little bit o' pest control, yer'll –' Schulze did a quick sum, his lips moving as he did so – 'yer'll have nearly a thousand of 'em nibbling away at yer armpits and crotch.' He beamed at the recruits, who were already wriggling and scratching as if they were infested by the 'little buggers'. 'There's many a time that I've had a good dozen of 'em eating away at my foreskin. Aint that true, Matz?'

Matz, who was in a sombre mood for some reason, nodded his agreement and took a slug of his firewater. Just as Schulze was going to cheer him up with his stories of the Russian rats that were 'as big as ponies', the loudspeakers above them under the bomb-shattered roof started to boom the final announcement, as far as the disguised SS Assault Regiment Wotan was concerned. '*Express to stop at Breslau, Konigsberg, Warsaw . . .*'

Schulze slung his fur-backed pack over his shoulder, as if

it were a kid's toy and said, 'Here we go, comrades.' Without waiting for the Vulture to give the regiment the order to get aboard, he cried, 'Make way for a rear admiral!' Giving the stationmaster in his red hat and black gleaming leather sash a shove, he was first, heading straight for the clean straw that lay in front of the glowing pot-bellied stove, feeling the heat blast his chilled face immediately with its delightful warmth.

Ten minutes later after the train had finally pulled out of the station and was gathering speed through the blacked-out surburbs, steadily heading east, the weary 'goodnights' started to come in from all sides of the compartment. At the stove, Schulze thrust in another log and wrapped his blanket around himself more tightly. A few moments afterwards he was snoring away happily, as were most of the old hares.

But there were many that night who couldn't sleep straight off. They lay on the hard floor, listening to the monotonous beat of the train's wheels, lost in dreams, their eyes trying to penetrate the red-glowing gloom of the carriage. Their minds were full of sombre shadows and dark forebodings. They were going up for the first time. They knew that. But what lay ahead of them in the ghost-ridden wastes of that dreaded country that awaited them, where so many young men like themselves had perished already? What indeed . . . ?

'*Ivans*!' the cry went up on all sides as the train lay panting like some exhausted beast just outside Konigsberg and the men were squatting at the side of the track to carry out their natural functions or attempting to wash their grubby faces and hands with melted snow. As the cry went up, Schulze, who had just bribed the engine-driver to give him a canteen of hot water from its boiler so that he could make hot tea to go with his rum, turned round to view the spectacle.

But even before he heard the shout and saw the strangers, he knew who they were. By their smell. There was no mistaking it. It was the same filthy stench as the monkey house at Hagenbek's Zoo in Hamburg to which his old mum had taken him as a kid before the war: a biting mixture of ordure, sweat and misery.

Now, the long line of skeletons in earth-brown uniforms, that of the Red Army, lurched towards the stationary train, urged on by elderly *Wehrmacht* guards on *panje* ponies, wielding their whips whenever necessary like cowboys riding herd in one of the wild-west films made in America.

As they came closer, the soldiers could see their faces were like death, hollowed out to skulls, from which eyes bulged, some of them so burning with hatred that the greenbeaks staggered back hurriedly, as for a fleeting moment they feared their flesh might be consumed by such a fire.

Schulze had little time for the Ivans, at least when they were armed. They were as cruel as some of their German enemies. They routinely killed wounded SS men who fell into their hands and their treatment of *Wehrmacht* prisoners was usually pretty cruel, shipping them off to the Gulag, where few of them survived the lack of food, the back-breaking work and the crippling cold. But this was different. The poor swine were totally at the mercy of their captors.

An emaciated giant with a blood-stained bandage wrapped round his head under his greasy fur cap, staggered towards the gaping greenbeaks, hands outstretched in the classic posture of supplication. '*Kleba* . . . *Kleba* . . . bread . . . bread,' he croaked.

One of the elderly guards, fat and brick-red in the face, urged his mount forward with his knees, wielding his whip cruelly as he did so. 'Back . . . back in the ranks, you Popov swine,' he urged. '*Himmelherrgott nochmal – zuruck!*' His whip curled mercilessly across the big Russian's back, drawing a line of bright-red blood.

'Stop, you bastard . . . stop that,' Schulze cried, almost dropping his precious hot water in a sudden rage. 'Or I'll stick that whip of yours so far up yer arse, yer glassy orbits'll pop out.'

The terrible threat worked and the fat soldier reined in his little mount, leaving the prisoner to stagger back to the column.

At that moment von Dodenburg felt proud of Schulze and the rest of his company. Like all SS men he felt no sympathy for the fighting Russian soldier, but he believed that defenceless prisoners should not be treated in such a manner. But five minutes later the lone guard on horseback bringing up the rear of the column to finish off stragglers with the pistol he held in his free hand, reined in his horse and said half amused and half apologetic, 'What's all the fuss about, comrades. They're only shitty Ivans, you know, mates. Not real human beings like you and me.' And with that he was off again, looking for more helpless victims, leaving the old hares to realize that they were almost back to the Russian front yet again.

That night as they passed into former Poland, they knew all too well that they had virtually reached that dangerous place from which so few men and boys like themselves ever came back.

Two

The night was very dark and the Vulture had posted sentries immediately, as the long train prepared to take on coal and water at this remote stop. They were still in territory controlled by Germany, but the guards at this lonely outpost consisted of two fat and frightened elderly reservists, wearing the ribbons of the First World War, who would probably lock themselves in their sandbagged hut once the train had departed. As the bigger of the two had told Schulze, who enquired of him, 'What do you do if you want a bit of the other out here, comrade?' 'A bit of the other! Those Polack partisans'd slice my love tool right off as soon as I got it out of my flies. We live dangerous out here in this arsehole of the world, sergeant,' he'd added with a quaver in his reedy voice.

Now as the wind swept across the snowy waste, the sentries froze. They huddled into their threadbare *Wehrmacht* greatcoats, breathing hard into their raised collars in a pathetic attempt to stop their dripping noses from freezing up.

In his compartment, which was still tolerably warm, though the temperature was sinking with the steam turned off, von Dodenburg studied the map. He was slightly puzzled. He had been outside to inspect the sentries, most of the greenbeaks obviously frightened and in need of reassurance; then he had taken a few minutes to study the stars. To him the constellations seemed to indicate that they weren't travelling in the direction he had anticipated: from Warsaw and then on to the central front in Russia. Now, as he stared at his map, it appeared to confirm his suspicion. If he'd got it right, they were now heading in a north-easterly direction. That would mean they were travelling in the general direction of the old

Russo-Finnish border, somewhere in the area of the long-besieged Leningrad. There, although the siege had been going on all throughout 1942, there had been no major action since the summer.

He let the map fall on to his lap. Outside, all was quiet save for the steady gurgle of water being pumped into the locomotive's tank and the solid crunch of the sentries' boots on the frozen snow. He pursed his lips in thought, his brow furrowed. The mystery of their destination and all this mumbo-jumbo that went with it was deepening. If they were really heading for a front where there had been no action for so long, why would they need the top-secret new Tiger tanks? Besides, if their move was connected with an attack on the besieged city, armour would be of little use to Wotan. Indeed he couldn't see the High Command risking those tanks in street fighting when some plucky youngster armed with a cheap bazooka might knock them out at close range. After all there was only a limited number of this 'war-winning weapon', as the one-armed SS colonel had called the Tiger, available.

His mind wandered a little, as he felt the chill rising from the metal floor and penetrating his boots and socks. He remembered those foreign officers at Grafenwöhr, who turned out to be their allies, the Finns. They had worked on the Tigers too, though he was certain the Germans wouldn't give them such a rare and precious fighting machine at this stage of the tank's development. Had they something to do with what lay before them?

But before a puzzled Kuno von Dodenburg could attempt to answer that particular question, a single shot rang out like a twig being snapped underfoot in a bone-dry wood at the height of summer. It was followed an instant later by a moan and the old cry, '*Sanitater . . . Sanitater . . . stretcher-bearer over here!*'

In an instant, all was chaos. Someone shrilled a whistle urgently. Schulze bellowed, 'Stand fast . . . Shoot anything that moves . . .' followed by the Vulture crying, 'Hold them . . . don't let them get near the locomotive. *Not the locomotive*!'

But as a ragged crackle of rifle fire broke out from the ranks of the sentries encircling the train, the cries of the attackers which von Dodenburg, hastily buckling on his pistol belt expected, didn't materialize. Instead, there was a strange panting noise which he couldn't identify and the sound of something racing across the frozen snow towards the stalled train.

He flung open the door to his carriage, pistol already clutched in his hand, safety off, ready to fire at a moment's notice. But the expected partisans weren't there. Instead, in the silver sheen of the stars, he could just make out half a dozen vague shapes, low and close to the ground, hurtling towards them.

For a moment he paused there, completely bewildered and then, in the light of the flare that one of the sentries had fired, as ordered, the shapes came into clearer view. 'Dogs!' he gasped.

Standing in the door of the next coach, the Vulture added, voice raised in sudden alarm, 'Battle dogs! . . . And look, von Dodenburg, they've got something attached to their backs.'

They had, and von Dodenburg recognized what their burdens were as they raced across the snow, heading straight for the officers' coach. A twin-pronged wire, whipping back and forth in the silver glare of the descending flare, was attached to a large bundle strapped to the dogs' backs and von Dodenburg recognized, with a sudden feeling of dread, what that bundle contained. He didn't wait for orders. Instead he cupped his hands to his mouth and cried urgently, 'Sentries, shoot the beasts . . . do you hear? Shoot to kill. They're carrying high explosive on their backs.' He raised his own pistol, snapped off a hasty shot – and missed.

His next one didn't. It caught a dog sinking to its haunches in an attempt to get underneath the coal tender, where the men shovelling coal were scattering wildly at the sight of the trained killer war dogs. For a moment nothing happened save the dog came to an abrupt stop, a red patch spreading rapidly across its light grey pelt. Then with dramatic suddenness, the bundle on its back exploded. The animal disintegrated. Its head flew through the air. Grotesquely it slapped against the side of the tender and slid down it, leaving a trail of blood behind.

Now the others took up the firing. Another dog was hit and exploded, leaving nothing behind save bits and pieces of bleeding flesh on the blackened surface of the snow. Still the dogs came on, trained ruthlessly to carry out their mission. One, wounded in the leg, was deflected from the locomotive, its objective. Instead it started to limp painfully towards the rear van of the train, which housed the machine-gun tower, permanently manned by troopers in leather clothing and masks to keep out the biting cold as they kept a lookout for partisans and the like. 'Hit that damned animal,' the Vulture called urgently.

Immediately half a dozen riflemen opened fire at the wounded animal. But it bore a charmed life. Slugs erupted all around it. Still it carried on, bearing its burden of sudden death. Now it was crawling. With any other animal von Dodenburg would have felt admiration for its bravery, obeying its unseen masters to the death. But not this one. This dog was the creature of a ruthless enemy.

The animal twitched as it was hit again. Blood spurted from a wound in its side. For a moment it stopped crawling. It was dying, von Dodenburg told himself. The danger was over. He was wrong. The dog rose somehow or other and continued its crawl of death. Now it was almost into the 'dead ground' where the bullets could no longer reach it. Up in his tower, the leather-clad figure of the young gunner stared down at the animal which intended to kill him in horror, as if he didn't know what to do.

Von Dodenburg cupped his hands around his mouth and yelled above the yelping of one of the dogs in its death throes, 'Throw a grenade, man!'

The warning died on his lips. It was too late and the young gunner was too petrified by fear to react, even if he had heard von Dodenburg's cry. Next moment it was too late for action. The dying dog crawled under the van. In that same moment it collapsed and, gasping frantically, succumbed to its wounds. In that instant the little twin-pronged aerial caught the van's steel axle. A tremendous boom. A ball of angry red flame.

The bundle of high explosive want up, tearing and ripping all before it.

The van seemed to rise from its bogies. A moment later it disappeared in smoke and flying chunks of wood as it disintegrated. The smoke cleared to reveal the headless gunner sprawled dead over his machine gun. The greenbeaks had had their first terrible taste of the kind of life that they faced now in the merciless war in the East . . .

Later that afternoon when the long troop train was finally able to continue its journey eastwards, Kuno von Dodenburg decided he would ask the Vulture the question which had been troubling him since he had been sent to Grafenwöhr and the events that had followed that posting. He had just finished presenting to the Vulture his official casualty and damage report as army regulations prescribed when it occurred to him that time for that overwhelming question had come. They were alone in the CO's compartment so that no one could listen to them and the Vulture seemed relaxed. He had loosened his collar, swung his boots on the seat and indicated that von Dodenburg should help himself to a drink from the bottle of *Korn* which balanced on the little table below the blacked-out window.

Fresh warmth was beginning to filter through from the locomotive and it was pleasant to sit there on the worn plush of the compartment reserved for officers after the biting cold outside. Indeed, even the rank-and-file appeared to be relaxed after the dog incident. Over the steady drumbeat of the train's wheels, von Dodenburg could hear someone playing the mouth organ and hearty voices joining in the chorus of '*Naughty Auntie Hedwig, who had been at her sewing machine all night and used up all her oil*.' The time and place were ripe, Kuno told himself as he raised his glass to the Vulture in toast, cried, '*Prost, Obersturm*,' and downed the fiery gin in one gulp that took his breath away for an instant.

In response the Vulture gave him a wintry smile and, encouraged by it, Kuno took the plunge. 'Sir,' he said, 'I've been studying the map this morning and I note we have changed direction.'

'Have we?'

'Yessir. Instead of going directly east, we are proceeding in a north-easterly direction.'

'So?'

'Well, sir . . .' Kuno hesitated momentarily and then continued with, 'Well, sir, if we continue on that course, I estimate we'll land either in the Leningrad Front.' At that moment something made Kuno add, 'Or on the Finnish front.'

The Vulture started visibly and Kuno realized he had touched a raw nerve. 'It does not do,' the CO said, 'for relatively junior officers to strain their brains and think too much. But let me tell you this much – in the strictest confidence, remember,' he added the warning. 'We are being sent to the Leningrad Front.'

'I see, sir,' Kuno answered routinely, but he knew that the Vulture was not telling the whole truth. 'But I wonder why the disguise.' He indicated the shabby *Wehrmacht* uniform he was wearing.

The Vulture shrugged with seeming carelessness and indicated that Kuno should help himself to another *Korn*. 'You know those nervous Nellies in Security and Intelligence, von Dodenburg. They probably think that the whole of the Ivan secret service is concerned with the movements of SS Assault Regiment Wotan. It'd be typical of them, wouldn't it? So they have to play their little tricks to conceal our transfer to the front. Now drink your drink.' He feigned a yawn. 'It's been a long day. I want to hit the hay.'

Hastily von Dodenburg drained his second glass and, rising, clicked his heels in salute before departing to his own coach, knowing as he did so that the Vulture had lied. There was more than this to it: a simple transfer of a single regiment to the Leningrad Front, which, for some obscure reason, Intelligence had attempted to conceal by making them change their SS uniforms for that of the *Wehrmacht*. The Vulture was leading them on some desperate venture that might well gain him those general's stars he coveted so much, cost what it may; and from the attack this morning it almost seemed that the Soviets knew they were coming.

Three

Together, General Govorov and the civilian Commissar Zhdanov rode through the dawn greyness in a motorized sledge, escorted by a troop of Red Army cavalry, bobbing up and down on their mounts, their drawn sabres resting on their shoulders, ready for action at a moment's notice. Govorov saw to their needs personally. He ensured they were fed well – their mounts too – and that they were never sent to the fighting front. They were there for his personal protection and he wanted them fit and totally loyal to himself.

This morning the two leaders had ventured out to the rear of the besieged city where the great Lake Lagoda offered the only means of entering Leningrad in an area now totally controlled by the Fritzes. Already the night's traffic, mostly raw infantry straight from the training depots, were forming up to march straight to the fighting front. Meanwhile the wounded from the previous day's skirmishes lay in the snow, most of them untended and hastily bandaged up, moaning and crying out for '*voda*'. For they were no longer of importance: they were incapable of fighting. They possessed the lowest priority for being evacuated across the Lake. The general told himself that a lot of them would die before the day was out; but then that was the lot of ordinary cannonfodder. He dismissed the thought and wondered why the civilian commissar, who he thought interfered too much in military matters, had been so insistent that he should come out here at this infernal hour and in such terrible weather.

Next him, the commissar, armed with a bottle of sixty proof vodka and wrapped in furs, was decidedly more optimistic than he had been when he had come to Govorov to plead for an attack on the 'Pimple'. 'Look at my people,' he said proudly, waving a gloved hand at a line of commissars haranguing the infantrymen, bellowing the usual patriotic slogans and the like against the background of a fresh artillery barrage. 'They'll get your soldiers moving, Comrade General . . . Put fire into their blood to win the Great Patriotic War.'

The General wasn't impressed. 'I wonder. A couple of priests blessing 'em might do more good. The footsloggers are simple folk. That's what *they* believe in.'

Zhdanov didn't take up the challenge. He was in too good a mood. 'Religion – the opium of the people,' he muttered and left it at that.

Now they were entering the shattered Leningrad suburb of Kolpino. Up to a couple months before, it had been part of the frontline itself. Now there were civilians back among the ruins who waved dutifully, if weakly, at the two important persons passing in the motorized sledge. Zhdanov waved back, smiling happily, but the general did not stir. He kept his hands covered by the warmth of the rich furs. He was still concerned with the civilian's reason for bringing him here, especially now as the thunder of the German artillery was getting ever louder. He scowled and made a quick calculation. The forward Fritz positions couldn't be more than four or five kilometres away. If the enemy decided to make a surprise assault from their nearest outpost, his Red Army cavalry wouldn't be able to stop them and he didn't like the thought of ending up in a Fritz prisoner-of-war camp. Not many Red Army men, even generals, survived those hellholes and even if they did, 'Old Leather Face' would ensure they were sent to the Gulag for having surrendered instead of fighting to the death, once they had been released.

Now the commissar indicated to the sledge driver he should slow down and turn to the left, where a group of civilians in overalls stood in front of a ruined factory, apparently waiting for them. The general eyed the place. The factory was without a roof, the girders twisted into grotesque shapes due to shelling, its brick walls pock-marked with shrapnel holes like the symptoms of some kind of loathsome skin disease. 'What is this place, Comrade?' he asked as the driver halted, the cavalry commander ordered his troops to stop and, as one, the civilians took off their greasy caps and bowed like the peasants had done in the old days in the presence of their overlords.

'The Izhrosky Industrial Plant,' Zhdanov announced, puffing out his burly chest, as if he had something here to be proud of. 'Here you'll see *my* tanks, Comrade General.'

'*Your* tanks!' the general breathed in exasperation. 'What damned tanks? The place is a goddam ruin.'

'Not quite, Comrade General,' the civilian answered in high good humour. He nodded to the factory workers. As one, they turned and, still carrying their caps in the manner of the humble peasants they had once been before their land had been taken away from them and they had been forced into the city and its factories – or starve to death, they trooped inside the apparent ruin.

They passed through what appeared to be a bomb-shattered workshop. There were broken lathes and smashed workbenches tossed in crazy confusion on all sides, with fading bloodstains adorning the whitewashed walls. The leading worker now stopped at what appeared to be a huge structure of rough planking plugging a gap in the wall. He knocked on it solemnly and, as the general watched in amazement, the structure opened like a door to reveal a women with cropped hair and carrying a tommy gun who eyed the new arrivals sternly. '*Stoi?*' she challenged like a regular Red Army sentry might.

'It's me, Katya,' the commissar replied and added (in the way that all these political civilians tried to show their closeness to the 'workers and farmers', the general couldn't help thinking), 'How is your man?'

The hard-faced female sentry remained very businesslike as she answered sternly and without any sign of emotion, 'He fell at the front yesterday, Comrade Commissar. 'You can pass.'

They stepped through the makeshift door and now the general could hear the electric hum of machinery and smell the heavy cloying odour of machine oil. 'What is this place?'

Zhdanov's smile broadened. 'As I have already told you, Comrade General. It is a factory – the Izhrosky Plant. In '41 the Fritzes bombed it out of existence. Now, as you see, the old factory has gone underground. Let me show you, *Davoi.*'

Still puzzled, the general followed the civilian commissar as he walked down a long sloping passage which led to a sturdy metal door, again guarded by a woman sentry – this one wore the beribboned cap of the Red Fleet – armed with a tommy gun. Once more they were challenged and the commissar passed some pleasantry before the door was swung open.

The noise hit the general in the face like a physical blow. It was tremendous. He actually flinched and closed his eyes momentarily before staring open-mouthed at the vast cellar that lay before him. It was packed with machinery, sub-divided by metal barriers into sections where hundreds of electric lathes hummed, drills ground through metal, sturdy workmen hammered metal and the tractor motors roared all out, spurting thick, stinking clouds of diesel fumes, as they generated the electricity needed to power all these machine tools.

The general pushed his cap to the back of his shaven head. '*Boshe moi*,' he exclaimed, 'I've never seen anything like this in my whole life, not even during the Revolution.' He stared pop-eyed at the scores of women working the lathes, their bodies wreathed in fiery blue sparks, sweat dripping down their faces from beneath the headscarves tied tightly around their hair.

'*Davoi*,' Zhdanov said joyfully, pleased with the impression he had made on the front commander. 'Now I show you why I brought you here, Comrade General. It is our pride and joy.'

Completely flabbergasted by what he had seen of this underground factory already, the soldier obeyed tamely and followed Zhdanov through yet another low, echoing cavern, packed with busy working people and stinking of oil, metal, stale black tobacco and human sweat. A moment later the commissar stopped dead, so that the general almost bumped into him. 'Now, Comrade General,' he said proudly, 'what do you say to those?' With a wave of his hand he indicated the six T-34s lined up to the rear of the workroom. 'Now then, isn't that a sight, eh?'

'Good God!' the general exclaimed, staring at the six tanks. Outwardly they didn't look much. A couple of them bore the silver stars of anti-tank rounds which had scored their sides, all of them lacked proper camouflage paints. But their guns were new and it was clear to the general's experienced eye that they were in running order. 'Where did you get them from, Comrade? At the moment you've got as many T-34s as my whole Front.' He whistled softly.

Zhdanov was only too eager to explain. 'They were abandoned on the battlefield during the great retreat in 1941, Comrade General. Either they had been hit and abandoned or they'd run out of fuel, so that their crews had to bale out and make a run for it. We acted before the Fritz reclamation crews could haul them away and use them themselves. It cost the lives of fifteen of our brave comrades to do so, including four women comrades. But we did it. We hid them here underground and then when the Fritzes were driven back at Kolpino, we uncovered them again and started working on them.' He indicated an ancient granny painting a red star on one of the powerful fighting machines. 'Everyone from Young Pioneers* to that babushka painting the star helped over long weary weeks. Now, Comrade General, they are yours. I feel you might have great need of them soon.'

The general shot him a sharp glance. 'What do you mean by that?' he rasped.

Zhdanov didn't answer immediately, for reasons known only to himself. Then he took the general by the arm and guided him out of the earshot of the others. 'There is a rumour,' he began slowly, as if he were still considering whether he should reveal the information he was now about to impart to the soldier.

'What kind of a rumour? After all, Comrade Commissar, there are always rumours at the front. It's part of our self-delusion.' He looked sharply at the civilian.

* Communist youth organization.

'It's not at the front, Comrade General,' Zhdanov said patiently. 'This comes from the rear, in particular Moscow, if you really want to know.'

'Yes?'

'It is that the Fritzes are up to something. They are shipping armour to this front apparently.'

'Armour to Leningrad in winter! Besides what use is armour in street-to-street fighting, as here in Leningrad?'

The civilian shrugged. 'I'm not a soldier. I don't know. But if the Fritzes are shipping armour here, one thing is for sure.'

'That is?'

'You'll need armour, too. *My* T-34s.'

The general was in no mood to congratulate the self-important civilian commissar. He contented himself with, 'I'm sure *your* T-34s will come in useful.' Then he turned and made his way outside again, his mind buzzing, wondering what the Fritzes were up to . . .

Four

'*Herr General*,' the burly middle-aged civilian with Gestapo written all over him said confidently, 'they maintain I can make even a mummy talk.' He laughed, showing his gold teeth. 'I have my methods, General. They've always worked so far, I can assure you.'

General Gehlen frowned. He had never really objected to using any means in order to obtain information. All the same, he disliked those used by the small Gestapo detachment attached to the headquarters of Foreign Armies East. He preferred traditional Intelligence methods: question and answer, the old 'sweet-and-sour' way used by two officers, even the dramatic confrontation in a darkened cellar with a bright light shining in the prisoner's eyes and blinding him. He detested the torture of the Gestapo. All the same he needed to know what their captive knew. It could be of vital importance for the planning of the future operation against the besieged Leningrad.

As if to hurry the general's decision, the Gestapo man pulled out a paper from inside his long ankle-length leather coat, which creaked audibly every time he moved, and handed it to Gehlen. 'From Reichsführer SS Himmler, General. He has given his authorization for the use of physical means.'

Gehlen looked at it. It read '*Strenger Arrest*'* and was signed by Himmler. He knew now that the matter was out of his hands. Himmler had ordered physical force. The Gestapo man could get on with it. '*Schon gut*,' he said, '*machen Sie weiter* . . . But I don't want to know the details. Just the *results*.'

* Severe Arrest. The formula which covered physical abuse. *Transl.*

The Gestapo man gave the general a crooked smile. 'Of course, sir. No one wants to know the details, do they? After all, mine is a nasty business, isn't it?'

Gehlen didn't reply. He hoped only that their prisoner was being kept in the deepest cellar of his HQ; he didn't want to hear the man's screams of pain when the Gestapo thug went to work on him.

The next moment, the Gestapo man touched his hand to his forehead in some sort of a salute and went. Outside, Gehlen could hear him asking, for some reason, if he could borrow a bucket. Gehlen frowned. Why in three devils' name did he want a pail? He told himself it was better than he shouldn't ask such questions; the less he knew the better.

The prisoner had been picked up by a routine check on the Berlin–Warsaw express. He had been wearing the uniform of an *Oberscharführer* in the Waffen SS. Normally his type of senior SS NCO wouldn't have been checked by Field Security. But this particular sergeant-major had been the strangest SS man they had ever seen: undersized and Oriental in appearance. Naturally the two Field Security men had known that there were SS units who were vaguely of Oriental origin employed in the Balkans against the partisans. But the sharper of the two security NCOs had noted the man had been wearing the armband of 'SS Wotan' – and that unit, the elite of the elite, Hitler's favourite, certainly wouldn't have had Oriental NCOs. They had decided to arrest the man for questioning. He'd pulled a concealed pistol and had shot the smarter of the two security NCOs. That had started the ball rolling.

Now he, Gehlen, was faced with deciding if the prisoner wearing the uniform of SS Wotan had anything to do with the sudden departure of that unit to Russia and the mission it would carry out there in the next days. It was a tricky problem. He daren't make too much fuss or the matter would be all over his headquarters; staff officers were often worse than old women in the way they gossiped. But at the same time, he had to know whether the secret mission had already been compromised.

In the cellar of the great house that had once belonged to some grand Russian nobleman before the Revolution, the Gestapo man prepared to find out that information for Gehlen. As he took off his leather coat, his jacket, and then rolled up the sleeves of his shirt to reveal hairy, brawny arms, a legacy of his days as a young butcher, he took a final drag of his cheap cigar and grinned at himself in the dirty mirror, which could be part of the torture. He was going to enjoy this, he told himself. It always gave him a sense of satisfaction when he managed to get some reluctant prisoner to talk; and in the end he always did. As he was wont to boast to his cronies, 'They either sing, comrades, or they'd better prepare to make a pretty stiff.' He called to his assistants in the small room to the right, 'Bring him in. I'm ready for the arsehole.'

The Gestapo man flashed a quick glance around the room, the floor a dull red with dried bloodstains and the stout chair set directly beneath the naked electric bulb which lit up the place. '*Los*,' he heard Karl, the chief assistant grunt, '*Auf die Beine*.' The command was followed by a groan as the prisoner was lifted from the concrete slab which had served as his bunk and dragged to his feet. Next moment the Gestapo man could hear the scrape of his boots as he was dragged across the floor. His grin broadened. He slapped one big fist into the open palm of his other hand, as if warming up for what was to come.

The smart SS sergeant-major who had been arrested on the Warsaw Express had been transformed into a dirty, bloody wretch. His uniform was covered with concrete dust from the bunk, his trousers were slipping around his knees for they had removed his belt so that he didn't try to commit suicide, and his face was a swollen mess of green and blue bruises where the Gestapo man's assistants had worked on it in a preliminary attempt to soften him up, after Gehlen's Intelligence officers had failed to get anything out of the stubby little man with the Oriental cast of features.

The Gestapo man spat out the stub of his cheap cigar. He spoke German, for, as he always said, 'Why learn any of those foreign lingos? Let 'em learn German. If they can't speak our tongue, so much the worse for the foreign bastards.' 'Just tell me what I want to know, old house, and then your suffering'll be over. There'll be a cancer stick, a cup of nigger sweat and a bite of grub for you. I'll give you to three.' He nodded to a grinning Karl, who knew what was coming. He went to collect the bucket.

Slowly the torturer started to count off to three, 'One . . . two . . . three.' He paused and then said, '*Los*, let's hear it. Who are you and what were you doing wearing the uniform of SS Assault Regiment Wotan?'

The prisoner's response was unexpected and surprised even the burly Gestapo man. The prisoner rasped and raised a gob of thick, yellow phlegm. The next instant he had spat the substance directly into the Gestapo man's face.

He staggered back, the liquid dribbling down his brick-red angry face. 'You dirty bastard!' he cried and without any further ado, he grabbed the bucket out of a surprised Karl's hands. Slapping it over the prisoner's head, he took up the broom that was propped against the wall. Next moment, exerting all his brutal strength, his muscles rippling beneath the thin fabric of his shirt, the slammed the broom handle against the pail. The blow was so hard that the prisoner was knocked completely off the stool on which Karl and the other assistant had placed him. As he fell, the bucket fell from his head to reveal that he was bleeding freely from both nostrils and from his ears.

The Gestapo man knew he could kill a prisoner this way if he continued to strike him in this manner. But his anger was so great that he was determined to continue the cruel torture until he felt the desire to cross-examine him. 'All right, Karl,' he ordered, 'put the arsehole back on the stool with the bucket on his turnip.' He spat on his horny palms, then seizing the broom handle prepared to strike once again . . .

'General.'

Gehlen looked up as his adjutant brought in the Gestapo thug. The latter was flushed with triumph and even at that distance Gehlen could smell the cheap *Korn* on his breath. He wrinkled his nose in distaste. Still he could tell the Gestapo man had got something out of the prisoner. He put down his pen and said, 'Would you like a cigar?', but he didn't ask the man to sit down.

'Thanks,' the other man said casually, 'I've got one.' He took the stub of his cheap cigar from behind his right ear and, without asking the general's permission, lit it. It was a provocation and Gehlen knew it, but he said nothing and waited.

The Gestapo man took his time. He fussed with the cigar deliberately, seemingly trying to get it to light properly. Then he could suppress his triumph no longer and burst out with, 'General, I got the little bastard talking, singing like a frigging yeller canary.' He beamed at the soldier.

'Did you now,' Gehlen responded icily.

'Yer. He's a major in the NKVD. He was dropped by parachute in Eastern Poland in late summer, smuggled himself into one of those Ivan POW camps there and then volunteered to become a *Hiwi* for us. Cunning bugger. Somehow he got himself into the Wotan regiment.'

Gehlen absorbed the information, while the Gestapo man sucked at his cheap cigar stump, rolling it from one side of his mouth to the other, almost as if challenging Gehlen to say he was wrong. Gehlen said nothing. His mind was on other things.

'Well, apparently he had a contact in Berlin who supplied him with plenty of money, gold to be exact, General. Probably in one of those so-called allied legations, Slovaks or Bulgarians. Those Slavs are all the frigging same. Anyhow, General, to cut a long story short, he bribed one of the Wotan officers—'

'*What*!' Gehlen sat up in his chair abruptly. That had struck home. 'Bribed an officer of the SS, you say. You have proof?'

The Gestapo man gave the startled general his crooked smile, obviously pleased he had made an impression at last. 'No sir. I've checked. The bastard committed suicide before the regiment left for the front. Name Dietz, *Hauptsturmführer*. Kept a high-class pavement pounder on the side and the whore needed money, plenty of it.'

Gehlen supressed a groan just in time. He didn't want the other man, the gross swine, to see any more of his weaknesses; a commander should never allow subordinates to be aware of his emotional failings. Could this Major Dietz, the dead man, have betrayed what he knew of the plan for the new offensive to the Russian agent? If so, something had to be done now. Or else. He snapped swiftly, 'I must talk with an interpreter to this Russian.'

The Gestapo man took out his cheap cigar and puffed a cloud of blue smoke in the direction of the alarmed general. 'Sorry, sir. But you can't.'

'Why?' Gehlen demanded sharply.

'Because, sir, the Ivan suffered a – er – sudden heart attack.' He winked knowingly.

'What?'

'Yessir, the Ivan's as dead as the swine he bribed to sell us out. I don't think he'll be doing much talking now . . .'

Five

'Would you follow me, gentlemen,' the guide who would take the First Company into the line requested politely, as if he were some kind of high-class domestic servant rather than a hardened old hare from an infantry battalion. 'The going'll be a bit tricky, but if you follow my instructions, I think we can make it without attracting any unwelcome attraction from the Ivans.'

Behind von Dodenburg and the Vulture, who had come up with him, Sergeant Schulze held his hand on his hip and wiggled his hips in a decidedly non-masculine fashion. In a fake falsetto he whispered to Matz, 'Give us a wet kiss.'

'Fuck off,' was Matz's reply. Old hare that he was, he didn't like what he saw one bit. There were dead everywhere, both German and Russian, and he knew from past experience, if the *Wehrmacht* dared not bury their own dead, this was going to be a very hairy section of the front.

'Oh, how crude you are, Corporal Matz,' Schulze simpered, but really his heart wasn't in it. He, too, realized that this was a very unhealthy place to be this December day. It was the same thought that occupied von Dodenburg's mind at that moment, as their guide, a woman's fur tippet wrapped around his neck to keep out the freezing, bone-chilling cold, said, 'Keep low, please, gentlemen. The Ivans have got an observation post at three o'clock near that wrecked *isba*.' He indicated the hut. 'And they're allus on the lookout for fool soldiers who don't watch what they're about.' He tugged the dewdrop from the end of his long red nose and flung it to the ground.

What were they doing here, the SS's premier regiment,

being wasted and suffering casualties probably before long, guarding a section of the front that any ordinary battalion of *Wehrmacht* stubblehoppers could take care of? Surely all this secrecy of the operation so far had not been meant for them to be used in this fashion? He looked at the Vulture, as if he half expected the CO to give him some sort of an explanation. But the Vulture's dissipated, hard face revealed nothing.

In fact the Vulture had been surprised himself when he had received the order to take Wotan into this section of the front, facing Leningrad. It had taken the scrambled phone call from no less a person than General Gehlen, commander of Foreign Armies East, to enlighten him. Swiftly the cold-faced Intelligence general had told him the reason for Dietz's suicide as gained from 'Igor', or whatever his real name had been. 'So this could mean, *Obersturmbannführer*, that the enemy might know all the details of your mission, though I doubt it somehow. However, one thing is certain – they know you're on the Leningrad Front. So we must try to convince them that you are there just like any other unit to take your turn in the line.'

'That will be difficult, sir, with the reputation that Wotan has as being the Führer's Fire Brigade. Why waste such a regiment as ordinary infantry?'

'I know, I know,' Gehlen had retorted, seemingly angry. 'But we have to try to convince the enemy that's the way it is. You will attack, as any new regiment does, and suffer a few casualties, bodies left on the field of battle. I'm hoping they'll believe that we are so short of infantry that we are bring forced to use you. After all, they'll soon identify the dead as being SS – SS from Wotan – by their blood group tattooed on their arms.'*

The Vulture hadn't been totally convinced. He didn't want to suffer any casualties if he could help it; he'd need every

* Unlike the soldiers of the *Wehrmacht*, the SS had their blood group tattooed on their arms so that if they were wounded, the medical officer would be able to give a blood transfusion more speedily.

man available for the operation to come. But orders were orders and he had left it there. Now he wondered who could be 'victims', probably the more undesirable of his regiment.

So the regiment moved forward, trying to keep hidden from the Russian observation post, sensing the heavy brooding silence of the snow-covered winter landscape. They filed by a gun crew dug in at the side of the rough track. But the gunners did not seem to see the new arrivals. They lounged around their gun, huddled up in their greatcoats, looking the other way. A little later, they came across the crews of two ambulances, camouflaged and hidden in a deep cutting at the side of the track. They were clustered around a fire, using smokeless fuel, warming their hands and smoking fitfully. Their conversation ceased when they saw the infantry filing by. It was the same with the cooks stirring pea soup in the great 'goulash cannon', as the portable stoves were called by the troops. They, too, looked sad, even ashamed as if they felt themselves somehow inferior to the infantry, snug, warm and well-fed as they carried out their humble task, knowing that they would survive long after the others were lying in the snow, dead.

Now they left the trail and started to work their way through blackened stumps of firs, with great brown shell holes everywhere. Here, too, there were the unburied dead, German and Russian, some of them locked in each others' arms, bayonets through their bodies like angry lovers entwined for ever. A German hung from a tree, dead, the remains of a fire below his feet where someone had attempted to defreeze them in order to steal the dead man's boots. Once they came across a big-bosomed Russian nurse, her army blouse ripped apart to reveal her great breasts. Someone had attached the little bells used by shepherds to prevent their flocks from wandering to each of the dead woman's nipples. With the weight of the soldiers tramping past, the bells began to tinkle happily. Von Dodenburg shook his head and one of the greenbeaks crossed himself hastily. Behind him, Schulze, suddenly very glum, said to no one in particular, 'The front . . . the shitting front . . .'

The men filing out of their trenches and dugouts to meet the relief were silent and watery-eyed, almost as if they might break down in tears at any moment. Most of them were clad in anything warm, mostly looted civilian bits and pieces, so that they looked like a crowd of motley civilians rather than soldiers.

Their CO, a one-armed major, came out from his command post, saluted the Vulture and eyed the tall, fit, young newcomers as if they were creatures from another world. Von Dodenburg told himself the *Wehrmacht* officer was wondering what a bunch of first-class troops were doing here where they'd soon be used up as cannonfodder, as had his own best soldiers. But he didn't ask. It was obvious he wanted to get away from this killing ground as soon as possible. It was always the same. Those being relieved didn't want to linger a moment more than necessary. The front swine were all convinced that their luck would then run out and they'd be hit before they escaped the hell of the front.

A corporal, dirty, undersized, bespectacled, who looked as if he might have been a village schoolmaster in civilian life, though his skinny chest was covered in decorations, looked up at one of the strapping giants who had just come up and said, 'Suppose you want to cover your manly chest with tin, eh?' He was referring to the medals that the German Army handed out so liberally. 'Well, you'll get plenty of 'em here, comrade, providing you don't get yourself shot too soon for Folk, Fatherland and Führer.'

The greenbeak looked down at the battle-worn corporal in bewilderment, probably wondering why he had been selected for this bitter attack from the front swine. 'I don't know . . .' he started to stutter but stopped as tears flooded the corporal's red eyes and he said thickly, 'Don't pay any attention to me, son. We're all *meschugge* –' he tapped his temple to indicate what he meant – 'up at the front. Good luck to you.'

Watching the front swine depart, staggering under their heavy loads of equipment and warm clothing, most of it looted civilian stuff, the men muttering and swearing to themselves like madmen, Corporal Matz muttered, 'Can't let that lot loose in civvie street now, Schulzi. They're a walking time bomb, danger to all and sundry.'

Schulze said nothing. He couldn't. For his part, von Dodenburg stared at their front, as the first Ivan flare sailed into the grey sombre sky, – the Russians were signalling that they knew there were newcomers facing them. For a few moments the snowbound countryside shimmered in that dazzling white light before the flare sank to the ground like a fallen angel, leaving the no-man's land between the fronts flooded with an eerie luminosity. For some reason he couldn't quite fathom, the tall blond officer shivered violently. The uncertain shadows out there seemed to suggest a world of silent ghosts. Then the Vulture's harsh voice cut into his reverie and brought him back to the harsh reality of the front. 'Officers Group in thirty minutes. Let's move it now!'

The Vulture didn't waste any time. Outside, the volume of Russian fire had increased ever since that first flare had sailed into the grey sky. It was clear that the Russians were testing the newcomers out – the old hares among the officers knew that and most of them hoped that the CO wouldn't do anything hasty in order to 'dominate the battlefield', as commanding officers were wont to put it.

At first, however, the Vulture contented himself with describing what faced Wotan to its immediate front. He explained that in the year and a half since Leningrad had been besieged by the *Wehrmacht* the Russians had built up formidable defences.

'The Ivans have three parallel lines. There is the fire trench, support trench and the communications trench. All are constructed in a dog-tooth manner. There are fire bays every ten metres so that bomb and shell blast are minimized. The bays also ensure that the defenders can't be enfiladed from the flanks in case our people break through. Naturally over that period of time the Ivans have been able to dig deep. Intelligence reports they've got to a depth of one and half metres with another metre of logs and sandbags on top on that.'

He paused and let the information sink in and by the look

on the faces of his listeners they were not particularly overjoyed by it. Then he continued with, 'The two other lines are even more formidable and complicated. The Ivans blasted great ditches into the permafrost with high explosive and their kitchens, stores etc. etc. are, in places, some three metres deep. Excellent defensive positions. We Germans couldn't have done better. You note I said *defensive* positions and I am sure that you have all heard Napoleon's adage that "he who defends a whole line defends nothing".'

Von Dodenburg started. He knew what that meant. The Vulture had some sort of plan of attack. He peered out through the slit in the bunker where the officer group was being held and told himself that if the Vulture did attack in strength, the Vulture could lose the whole damned regiment in a single morning against those kind of defences. But the Vulture had other plans in mind for the men of Wotan. 'So having said all that, gentlemen, let me tell you in absolute confidence that I do not think Wotan will be staying for many days. Personally I'll give it a week at the most.'

There was a gasp of surprise from the assembled officers. It was an announcement that they had not expected one bit. The Vulture appeared not to notice their reaction. Instead he went on immediately, saying, 'But we must make it clear to the Ivans that we are present on this section of the front. Naturally they know that a new unit has moved in. I want them to know that.'

Again his listeners exhibited surprise and again the Vulture didn't seem to notice. 'To make quite sure that they *do* know we are here, I'm preparing a minor sally on their position. Nothing major, resulting in large-scale casualties – Wotan cannot afford to lose too many men.' He paused and added a cynical smile on his ugly horsey face. 'Not yet at least.'

For the moment von Dodenburg ignored the CO's cynicism; he was too glad that the Vulture was not going to launch a major action with a lot of casualties.

'I intend to attack tomorrow night at the time the Ivans usually stand down for the night. We'll penetrate the Ivans' first line of defence and take out one of their bays. With a bit of luck we'll find a company HQ so that we can grab maps and prisoners for Intelligence. But the results are not so important; it will be the penetration and the fact that we have done it that count. Now I'd like to use half a company at the most—'

'I'll volunteer my First Company, sir,' von Dodenburg cut into his words.

Slowly the Vulture shook his head. 'Not you, von Dodenburg. Some of your company perhaps. Sergeant-Major Bulle will select the men I need. But you will report to HQ at eight hundred hours tomorrow morning. The order just came through.' The CO touched his gloved hand to his cap and said, 'That will be all for the time being.' He turned without another word, as they snapped hastily to attention, and went out, leaving von Dodenburg puzzled beyond measure.

BOOK FOUR

The Finnish Connection

One

The Army Group Headquarters was in a flap, Kuno von Dodenburg could see that. The normally leisurely staff officers, some with the red stripe of the Greater German General Staff running down their elegant, tailor-made breeches, were striding to and fro hurriedly. All seemed to be carrying important-looking documents. Some were discussing whatever was going on with each other in low, excited whispers. From the little room off the main corridors, there came the urgent jingling of telephones, the whirr of duplicating machines and the clatter of typewriters. Even the smart 'officers' mattresses', as the Army's female auxiliaries were nicknamed by the front swine, no longer lounged and did their nails or applied more lipstick to impress some senior officer, but went about their duties, as if they really meant business.

Still the usual routine of a major headquarters continued. Kuno von Dodenburg had to show his pass six times from arriving in the snow-heavy courtyard outside till he was received by a haughty-looking military police captain at the top of the corridor, who examined his papers as if he might be a Russian spy before snapping, 'All right, *Hauptsturmbannführer*, office to your right. They're waiting for you.'

'Who—?' he attempted to find out who 'they' were, but the police captain cut him off with a sharp, 'You'll see soon enough.'

Von Dodenburg flushed and told himself the staff officer would have changed his tune if he had been wearing his uniform as an officer in SS Wotan, but the man was already examining someone else's papers. He knocked on the door indicated and after a pause went in. '*Grosser Gott*,' he began, taken completely by surprise, then remembering military courtesy, he touched his hand to his cap and saluted, muttering, '*Guten Tag*.'

A tough-looking Finnish officer from Grafenwöhr, who hadn't appeared to speak any German in Bavaria, rose to his feet and advanced on a totally flabbergasted Kuno, saying in excellent German. '*Ach mein lieber Herr von Dodenburg. Sie kennen mich noch, was*?'

'Yes, I know you, sir,' he stuttered and took the Finn's hard paw.

The Finn beamed and, relinquishing Kuno's hand, turned and introduced the others in the room. They were all Finns, dressed in their distinctive khaki uniform, save one, wearing what von Dodenburg took to be a naval tunic. More surprisingly the Finn wearing the blue uniform was a woman: a somewhat plumpish woman with platinum-blond hair neatly tugged beneath her cap with its tarnished gold braid, her face bronzed and very healthy looking. Indeed, despite her smallness, she might have been one of those beautiful, superfit Baltic blondes whom Kuno remembered from the travel posters of the early thirties: posed on some white-sand beach, holding a ball, standing on the tips of her toes to display an excellent figure.

'Captain Gunnerson,' the Finnish major said, 'a member of the Death Squadron.'

What the 'Death Squadron' was, Kuno von Dodenburg had no idea or interest in at that moment as the female naval officer flashed him a beautiful white-toothed smile: he was completely absorbed with her face which radiated the kind of total health that he had not seen in a German woman for years now. For her part, the captain said in good German, 'Ach, the hero of SS Assault Regiment Wotan.'

Kuno von Dodenburg actually blushed.

The Finnish major, however, frowned. He said something in Finnish and the woman was suddenly very serious again. Kuno took it he had reprimanded her for speaking the name of Wotan. Then he got down to business.

'*Herr von Dodenburg*, I think you have wondered what all

this is about. Grafenwöhr and your splendid Tiger tanks. The move of Wotan to the Leningrad front, disguised as soldiers of your fine *Wehrmacht*.'

Kuno nodded. He disregarded the Finnish major's praise of German arms. After all he belonged to a very small nation fighting a giant. His country needed a powerful ally like Germany to win the one-sided struggle. 'Yes, I admit I have.'

The Finn smiled at him and the others, who obviously understood German, too, did the same encouragingly. 'Well, most of the secret can be revealed to you now, though of course I do not know the fine detail of our generals.' He allowed himself a faint smile. 'But then who does know what really goes on in the mind of generals, eh?'

There was a murmur of agreement and the Finn went on. 'Your General Lindemann' – the commander of all German troops on the Leningrad front – 'has been ordered to take Leningrad before the Reds start their spring offensive. The Finnish forces will join him in this attack by our German comrades. To help the Finnish attack, the Führer has agreed to allow your Wotan to assist us in a seaborne attack.'

Kuno started. '*Seaborne*?'

'Yes. We Finns have great experience of the Gulf of Finland and the Lake Lagoda waterways.' He nodded to a tall captain, who carried one of the small curved knives at his belt like the first Finns Kuno von Dodenburg had met at Grafenwöhr. Hastily, he unrolled the map he had under his arm and spread it on the table in front of then. They crowded closer and stared down at it as the Finnish major continued with his briefing. 'The main German forces will attack between Pulkova and Mga – here and here. We think that is the junction between the two Russian armies holding the Leningrad front. It is also, as you know, usually the weakest point on any front held by two armies.'

He let the information sink in and went on with, 'We Finns will do our best to help with a seaborne attack out of the Gulf of Finland on the left flank of General Lindemann's force. Your regiment, Herr von Dodenburg, with your Tigers, will spearhead our attack. Our – *your* – objective will be to cross the peninsula there and reach the nearest point at Lake Lagoda. Hold that objective and we cut the Russians off from their own source of supply. Lindemann's men will be able to attack without fearing the Russians will bring new men and new supplies across the Lake to aid the defenders.' He straightened up and smiled around the circle of young excited faces. 'With luck, Leningrad will be in our hands as a Christmas present for your beloved Führer.'

Kuno von Dodenburg smiled with them, but he was still puzzled. 'But how are we to get sixty-ton Tiger tanks across the Gulf of Finland to this place Straina?' he asked.

The Finnish major turned to the platinum-blonde naval officer. 'Please tell him,' he commanded.

'We have developed landing barges since we first heard of your new tanks,' she explained, dazzling Kuno with those beautiful teeth of hers. 'They will carry your tanks – and you of the Wotan.'

'Such barges could be an easy target,' Kuno objected.

'Not when they are escorted by the ladies of the Death Squadron and their fast craft,' the Finnish major cut in. 'Now I shall leave you, *Hauptsturmführer*, to discuss the matter further with Captain Gunnerson.' He looked at his watch hastily. 'I'm hoping that General Lindemann will be able to see me in five minutes. There are lot of details still to be discussed. *Gentlemen*!' The Finns clicked to attention and bowed. Kuno returned the bow and then they were gone, leaving him standing there rather awkwardly facing the blonde, wondering how he was going to deal with her; from the medal ribbons on her splendid chest she was obviously some kind of fighting woman and a member of this strangely named 'Death Squadron'.

But if he had inhibitions, the Finnish woman hadn't. She took his hand and said gaily, her pretty healthy face wreathed in a huge smile. 'Come on, Herr von Dodenburg, don't look so glum. Let's get out of this place and go to the sauna.'

'*Sauna*?' He had first encountered the sauna back in summer 1941 when the *Wehrmacht* had first invaded Russia. He had learned it was a first-class means of getting clean and rejuvenating a weary body after battle. But he had never heard of a woman using the bath at the same time as a man. 'It is a strange place for a conference or briefing,' he heard himself saying.

She winked and lowering her voice said seductively, 'Perhaps we can do more there than talk, Herr von Dodenburg . . .'

'Frig this for a game o' soldiers,' Schulze growled, as the little group dropped into the hole, while the Russian mortars tore the sky apart with an obscene howl. 'Comrades, I think this is gonna be an Ascension Day Commado* if we don't watch out.' To their immediate front the snowfield heaved and erupted in a shower of earth. Pebbles pattered down on the men's helmets.

'Yer can say that again, Schulzi,' Matz shouted as the mortar shells exploded one after another, buffeting their faces like a blow from a soft wet palm. He raised himself above the rim of the hole and loosed off a quick burst from his machine pistol at the skeletal tree to his right where he suspected the artillery observer, directing the mortar fire, might be hidden. A scream and a body slammed to the ground and lay still. Matz had been right. Still all of them, old hares that they were, knew they had been spotted already. Soon another observer would start directing the Ivans' fire on to them.

It had been the Bull who had selected them in what he thought was his usual humorous way. 'The CO needs volunteers for a special mission,' he had announced earlier that day, breath fogging the icy air. He had favoured them with his big-toothed smile and added, 'You . . . you . . . you and you. You've all volunteered. The CO knows he can rely on his front swine from the First Company to do the job properly . . . There's a bottle of vodka for each of you when you get back. The CO's promised that.'

'*If* we get back,' one of the old hares selected had moaned.

'Well, you don't want to live for ever, do you?' the Bull

* A mission of no return. *Transl.*

had responded cheerfully. 'Enjoy life and then make a handsome corpse, that's what I allus say.'

'I hope that his frigging Hannalore's pregnant by me so that he'll be haunted by us Schulzes till the end of his days,' Schulze had growled. 'Then *he* can make a handsome corpse, the bastard!'

Matz had looked at his old running mate curiously after they had been dismissed by the Bull to prepare for their mission into the Russian lines. 'What's wrong?'

'Can't you see, Matzi? The bastard has gone and picked all old hares for this job – and all of them he thinks are troublesome, including me and you. Now we're supposed to go out there and nab an Ivan prisoner for Intelligence. What intelligence? And why a prisoner? The big shots already know who's opposing us on the other side of that line. Why send out a patrol of ten odd old hares like us?'

'Go on, tell me, Schulzi. I'm all ears.'

'I know you are. They stick out like bloody cup handles. Why, because he doesn't want us to come back. He wants us to make handsome corpses . . . get rid of us trouble-makers while Captain von Dodenburg is out of the way.' He shook his head angrily. 'Great crap on the Christmas Tree, I bet the Vulture's behind all this.'

Now after the mortar bombardment had ceased, a Russian machine gun started to sweep the snowy waste ahead of the little patrol with tracer fire. The Russians were obviously seeking them out. Carefully, very carefully, Sergeant Schulze raised his head above the rim of the hole in which they were sheltering and surveyed the scene. Behind, his little command waited anxiously. They knew the Russians would pinpoint them sooner or later; then all hell would be let loose.

Schulze, sweeping his gaze rapidly from left to right, heard Dietrich, an old hare, who had already been wounded twice in Russia, snarl, 'We've walked into a trap, comrades. Why don't we just surrender and get it over with.'

Schulze's face hardened. 'Arse with ears – *surrender*, you say!'

'We're in *Wehrmacht* uniform, Schulze,' Dietrich said, as

a fresh burst of tracer kicked up spurts of snow to their rear and the trapped men told themselves the Ivans were getting closer. 'They won't do anything to us except a good kick in the arse and a bit of punching.'

'*Nothing to us*,' Schulze sneered, brain racing as he tried to find a way out of the impasse. 'Haven't you got any cups in yer frigging cupboard? As soon as the Ivans see that SS blood group tattoo of yourn, you're for the high jump in zero, comma, nothing seconds. Man, use yer frigging head.' He stopped short. Under the cover of the machine-gun fire, Russians, armed with round-barrelled tommy guns, were coming in from the left flank. Time was running out. He had to make a decision – and make it quick.

Two

While Schulze wrestled with himself to make a decision about what he and the apparently doomed patrol should do, von Dodenburg, his company commander, had the decisions made for him. The blonde Finnish girl led him into the sauna, guiding him to the door by the hand, as if he were some reluctant young man heading for his first sexual encounter; and he was sure that was what she had in mind with him. For her whole being exuded sex and desire.

At the door, she stopped and without a word, started to take off her uniform and piled it neatly on the wooden door next to the entrance. When, after a moment, she was already stripped to her knickers, revealing a pair of splendid breasts, she said in her accented but delightful German, 'Come on, *Obersturmbannführer*, don't be shy . . . Take off your clothes.'

Von Dodenburg, who had had sexual experiences with women of a dozen different races since the war had begun, was not in the least shy in such matters. But as he told the half-naked blonde, 'This is the habit in your country, but not in mine. It is difficult.'

She laughed out loudly, almost in the manner of a man and boomed, 'Naked bodies are the same the world over. Now, please, we have not much time and the firewood supply is limited. Take off your uniform.'

Minutes later they were completely naked and shrouded in hot steam as she poured more and more water over the glowing wood coals. It was a strange feeling for Kuno to be alone in this wooden shack with a completely naked woman whom he had met only hours before. But she was completely uninhibited. She moved around the place when it was necessary without any attempt to conceal her hairy loins, her fine breasts, the broad dun nipples erect with the heat – and perhaps sexual excitement for all Kuno knew – swinging slightly as she did so in a way that was totally provocative. In a way this uninhibited parading of her sexual charms embarrassed Kuno, for it was too exciting and at times he was forced to hide his growing tumescence. Not that that worried her. For twice as the steam parted for a while and she spotted how excited he was, she leaned over, flipped his hardness with her thumb and forefinger as if testing its strength, saying in that throaty voice of hers, 'Soon.' And Kuno von Dodenburg didn't need a crystal ball to know what was to be 'soon'.

Yet seemingly she was not ready for the culmination of this strange business of the sauna. Once she rushed out, giggling hugely, her strong fleshy buttocks swinging from side to side delightfully, and flung herself full length in the deep snow. Turning herself round and round in it like an excited child till her body glowed a bright red, she came rushing back and started beating her steaming red body with twigs, as the steam rose yet once again.

It was almost too much for Kuno. He felt he had to take her soon or he'd burst with sexual desire. But when he did, it came in a different fashion than he had imagined these last few minutes. Abruptly she turned, her healthy open face abruptly very serious. Wordlessly she handed him the bundle of twigs with which she had been beating her body. He looked at them and then at her.

Suddenly he realized what she wanted him to do to her and as if she could read his thoughts, she nodded and then, spreading herself full length on the wooden bench, waited.

For what seemed an age, though probably it was only a matter of seconds, Kuno hesitated. He had heard of such things, but never in his wildest dreams had he thought he would ever be involved in them. She wriggled her plump buttocks in invitation and moaned. Suddenly he was seized by a desire to hurt her; he didn't know why. He took the bunch of twigs and slapped it down across her bottom. She groaned. But it was of pleasure not pain. 'More!' she gasped.

He swung the bunch of twigs down once more and this time he struck even harder. She writhed, raising her buttocks and then slapping her wet stomach against the bench, muttering something in her own language. He hit her again with all his strength. He was sweating heavily now and sexually excited more than he had been for a long time. He *wanted* to hurt her. He wanted to make her scream. Then he wanted her.

Moments later the two of them were writhing on the floor like crazy animals, gasping and choking, biting and clawing at each other, more like deadly enemies than lovers, carried away by a kind of passion of hate which wanted to inflict pain not give pleasure. It left them sprawled on the wet floor, panting madly like two individuals who had just run a long, hard race. Then as the heat started to die away as the steam vanished and their supply of logs dwindled to nothing, their breathing slowly returned to normal. All passion spent, Kuno whispered, 'I'm sorry . . . I didn't want to hurt you . . .' He frowned, trying to find the right words to express his feelings. 'I don't know . . . Suddenly I was carried away. For God knows what reason . . . I just wanted to hurt you.'

She reached across. Gently she ran her knuckles down his cheek. 'I know, I know . . . It is my fault. I made you do it.'

He sat, resting his head on his hand, and gazed down at her body, the splendid breasts seemingly smaller now as they fell to either side of her chest, the nipples flat and no longer excited. 'You're a funny woman . . . God, I don't even know your name!'

'Christiana.'

'Well, you are, Christiana. Why do you want such things? Why be hurt, eh?'

She shrugged slightly. 'Perhaps I need to be hurt . . . punished. And –' she gave him a trace of that beautiful, brilliant-toothed smile of hers – 'I enjoy it, too.'

For a moment or two the conversation palled. They dressed and headed back to the HQ. They could hear the drumbeat of the permanent barrage now and somehow it seemed to Kuno's trained ear that it sounded louder now. Something was on the way; that explained the flap at General Lindemann's HQ.

'Why do you need to be punished?' he asked after a while, his mind occupied with the strange behaviour of the girl he had just made love to and the increased noise of the artillery bombardment.

She thought about it for a while before saying slowly, as if she were just making up her mind at this very moment, 'Perhaps it's because I belong to the Death Squadron . . . because I send other women to their deaths, when they should be in love, making babies, doing things that women are supposed to do when they are young.'

He looked at her, puzzled. 'Sending women to their death? . . . What is this Death Squadron of yours?'

Before she could answer, the same supercilious military police officer who had examined von Dodenburg's papers when he had first entered the HQ came hurrying down the corridor to where the two of them waited on a bench for further orders. '*Haupsturmführer*,' he called urgently. '*Hauptsturmführer* von Dodenburg.' He lowered his voice suddenly as he realized that the SS officer was wearing the shabby *Wehrmacht* uniform, which was Wotan's cover. 'Trouble . . . trouble with your regiment.'

Kuno forgot the girl and her problems. He sprang to his feet swiftly. 'What is it?'

'We've just received word. One of the patrols from your company has been reported missing. Naturally HQ is worried that they may have been taken prisoner and identified as . . .' he lowered his voice to a whisper, 'as Wotan. The staff thinks—'

'What in three devils' name has happened?' Kuno von Dodenburg cut him off sharply, every inch the arrogant SS officer, who showed no respect for members of the *Wehrmacht*, whatever their rank, 'Tell me.'

The MP captain repeated his message. Kuno didn't hesitate. He turned to Christiana. 'We'll meet again,' he snapped. 'Now I must go. My men are in trouble, you understand.'

She nodded, her eyes suddenly wary, he thought. But Kuno had no time to consider the Finnish girl's feelings now. His men were in danger – how and in what way he didn't know – and he had to do his best to help them. As always, Wotan and its men came first. Without another word, he turned and went, leaving her and the problem of this strange sounding 'Death Squadron' still not explained . . .

Schulze had done his best. So far his little band hadn't suffered any casualties, save for Dietrich, who had been shot in the left arm, so that he was still able to use his rifle. But the big NCO knew his luck could run out at any moment. For now the Ivans were behind him, too. They had attacked suddenly, and the patrol had been caught completely by surprise by the first nerve-shredding *brhh-brehh* of a Russian tommy gun to their left rear. It had been then that Dietrich had been wounded. But the tommy-gunner hadn't lasted long. Swiftly Matz had pulled the stick grenade from his boot and in the same moment had hurtled it at the approaching Russians. The tommy gun had clattered down to the frozen snow as the Russian seemed to disintegrate, his head, complete with helmet, rolling away like some ball abandoned by a careless schoolkid.

Then for a few minutes, though it seemed to the surprised SS troopers like an age, a savage firefight had raged. Scarlet flashes of flame had stabbed the grey gloom on all sides. Grenades sailed back and forth. A soldier ran at Schulze with his bayonet fixed, yelling his head off. 'Try this one on for size, you Popov piss-pansy,' the big noncom had snarled and had given him a burst from his Schmeisser. At that range Schulze couldn't miss. The Russian took the burst in the stomach. He fell screaming, '*Matka*!' But there was no mother to help him in this place of sudden death. His stomach falling into the cradle he made of his arms, oozing from his ripped-open belly like a steaming grey and red snake, he hit the snow. Behind him, another Russian was hit. He whirled around furiously like some Cossack dancer. He went down, too. A minute later the steam went out of the Russian attack. They dropped to the ground, while a desperate Schulze's mind raced as he tried to find some way out of the trap in which the patrol now found itself.

Schulze knew that they couldn't go to ground. That would

be fatal; they would be playing into the hands of the attackers. They had to keep on the move.

But which way? Now the Ivans lay to his front and rear. It had been then that he had made his decision. He had reasoned that the enemy would expect him to back off, try to fight his way to the rear and his own lines. He might, however, catch them off guard – at least for a while – by doing the exact opposite. He'd push on to his front, right into the heart of the Russian defences. It was the kind of shock tactic which SS Wotan was used to. The Russians, on the other hand, were ponderous and slow in their tactical thinking.

Now, a desperate Schulze and his collection of old hares were doing just that. And for the time being it was working. The Russians hadn't expected this handful of veterans to react in this manner. Here and there a soldier popped up from his slit trench and attempted to fire at the dirt-covered gasping old hares. But the veterans were quicker off the mark. Now they were through the first trench line, leaving behind a trail of dead and dying Russians to mark their deadly progress.

But to the rear of the first line where the supply and support trenches lay, the Russians were finally beginning to react. Flares were sailing urgently into the air. In their old-fashioned manner, for the Russians possessed little radio equipment even in their tanks, signallers were standing on the tops of bunkers hurriedly wiggling their flags for support from other bunkers.

Ducking and sprinting, trying to ignore wild volleys of small-arms fire, Schulze in the lead sought frantically for the safest way ahead. But it was damned difficult and highly dangerous, especially as Schulze's height and position at the head of the escapers made him the obvious leader: the one any Russian sniper would want to bring down first of all.

Then Schulze saw what he needed. The realization that this was perhaps the only way out came to him instantly with the immediate certainty of a vision. To the left some hundred metres away, two stationary tanks appeared abruptly out of the snow which had begun to fall once more, thickening by the minute. He saw his chance at once. Veering sharply to the left, he cried above the angry snap-and-crack of the small-arms fight. 'T-34s at ten o'clock. Near bunker! *Mir nach, Manner!*'

They needed no urging. They changed direction at once, all of them having implicit faith in the big Hamburger's ability to get them out of the sorry mess in which they found themselves.

'*Stoi*?' the challenge came suddenly in Russian. A man clad in overalls and wearing the leather helmet of a tank crewmember appeared out of the white-out. He pulled out his pistol and aimed with amazing slowness, as if this were a training exercise and not the real thing.

Schulze thought and acted differently. Before the Russian tanker could fire, Schulze slammed his Schmeiser against the muzzle of the pistol. It fell from the man's abruptly nerveless fingers and the two of them tumbled to the snow. A broad unshaven peasant face stared up at Schulze. Not for long. Schulze smashed his fist like a small sledgehammer down on the Russian's face. The man's nose broke. The Russian howled in agony as Schulze smashed his fist down cruelly once more. And again. The Russian gave a little whimpering sound, the blood pouring over Schulze's red-raw knuckles, and then the man's head lolled to one side and he lay still in a star of his own blood, either dead or unconscious; Schulze didn't care which. Schulze was concentrating on the two T-34 tanks. 'Get aboard,' he yelled. 'Sodding *dalli* now . . . into those tin cans at the double . . .'

Three

'*Heaven, arse and cloudburst!*' von Dodenburg exploded. 'What's going on?' He glared at the Vulture, who returned his look in that icy supercilious manner of his, appearing to be staring the excited young officer down through his monocle.

Outside, in the Russian lines, ever more signal flares were soaring into the grey sky and from both flanks the enemy was firing machine guns interspersed with the occasional artillery round, as if the Russians were expecting an attack from either flank.

'That is no way to address your commanding officer, *Hauptsturmführer*,' the Vulture said coldly, taking out his monocle and polishing it slowly, as if he had all the time in the world.

Von Dodenburg knew he hadn't. For already he knew that part of his First Company under the command of Sergeant Schulze had disappeared somewhere behind the enemy lines. 'For God's sake, why Schulze and my old hares? What was the purpose of it all?'

'Someone had to go. They were the most experienced troops under my command.'

'But to what purpose, sir, I repeat?'

'To provide the evidence that the Greater German High Command wants to prove to the Russians that Wotan is here on this part of the front and will remain here. You know, von Dodenburg.'

Kuno looked at the Vulture aghast. 'But you can't use men – my men, in particular – in some kind of intelligence game. It's . . . beyond . . . belief.'

'Is it? What does their fate really matter, von Dodenburg? They're front swine, aren't they? If they're not killed today, then they'll be killed tomorrow.' He shrugged. 'It's always been like that, you must know, you – I – are front swine as well.'

At the back of his head a cynical voice said to Kuno: Brave the Vulture may be and he *is* a front swine, but he's one who is intent on surviving. But even in his present blinding rage, he daren't say that aloud to the Vulture's face. The CO wouldn't hesitate in having him courtmartialled for insubordination. So he controlled himself with an effort and asked as calmly as he could: 'What do we know of the Schulze patrol, sir?'

'Not much really. The sergeant took out a dozen men with him. The objective was to bring back a Russian prisoner for identification purposes.'

Von Dodenburg caught himself just in time. What a damned fabrication that was. They already knew what Russian division faced them here. The supposed objective was intended only to get the men on the patrol killed or captured so the Ivans could identify them as members of SS Assault Regiment Wotan.

'And then, sir?' von Dodenburg prompted.

'Our forward listening positions heard firing – our own and that of the Russians. It was obvious that the patrol had run into the enemy. Since then, well, the Russians are still firing, as you can hear. But there's no sound of our own weapons.'

Von Dodenburg said nothing. For a moment he didn't know what to do. For the want of anything else, he peered through the slit in the sandbagged bunker. The flares were still exploding in the sky to his front where the Russians were and a little further back the grey sky flickered with bright-red forked light, almost as if a summer storm was brewing in the middle of winter. Faintly he could hear the sound of tank cannon. He frowned. What did that mean? There were no German tanks on this front. Why should the Ivans be firing tank cannon? Then he dismissed the matter. There were things to be done. His rage had subsided. Still, if he could do anything about it, he was not going to allow the Vulture to sacrifice his old hares – Schulze, Matz, Dietrich and the like – for the sake of some damnfool intelligence ploy. Besides he had a sneaking feeling that the Vulture had made the Bull pick the most insubordinate of the old hares for this patrol. He turned and faced a waiting Vulture. 'Sir, can I have your permission to attempt to find out what has happened to my men?'

The Vulture took his time. He answered von Dodenburg's question with one of his own. 'But why risk your life for the sake of a handful of men who are not much better than cannon-fodder?'

'They are the men of my First Company, sir. I don't think that the men will respect an officer who doesn't try to help his soldiers when they are in trouble, do you, sir?' He looked straight ahead, almost as if he were standing on parade.

The Vulture flushed a little. The statement had hit home. He knew that he had achieved respect not through example, but through fear. His men hated and were frightened of him. At the same time as these thoughts went through his head, the Vulture realized yet again how little this damned arrogant officer standing in front of him now as the bunker shivered and trembled like a live thing under the impact of the Russian bombardment respected him. Why shouldn't he get rid of von Dodenburg, the supercilious swine, just as he had done the old hares, an insolent bunch of rebels? He made his mind up. 'All right, *Hauptsturmbannführer*, if you want to risk your neck for sake of that bunch of insubordinate pig-dogs, you may.' He shrugged. 'It's up to you.'

Von Dodenburg straightened to attention and touched his hand casually to the brim of his rakishly tilted cap. 'Thank you, sir. I'll go immediately.'

The Vulture returned the salute and remarked, 'Then let it be on your head, von Dodenburg.' He returned the younger officer's salute and then turned his back on him, as if peering through the slit in the sandbags. It was as if von Dodenburg no longer existed for him . . .

The Russians had discovered the German enemy in their midst only minutes before. Matz had taken control of the first T-34 and, expert tank driver that he was, had soon familiarized himself with the new Russian tank's very simple controls. Schulze had done the same with tank two, leaving Hansen, the big Northerner, to slip into the driving seat which was meant for a much smaller man. As usual with the Soviet tanks there was no radio contact between tanks, but before they had 'buttoned up', pulling the hatch down, he had come up with a simple means of signalling with Matz. They'd use the tank headlights to signal 'forward', 'reverse', 'to left and right', etc. etc. Then they had closed their respective turret hatches and got down to making a plan of escape before the Ivans discovered their presence.

But they had not had the chance to complete them. For peering through the commander's slit in the T-34's turret, Schulze had seen how a small patrol of Russians had come across the dead tanker, who had guarded the tanks and whom they had killed. For what seemed a long time the Ivans had peered down at the man slumped in the snow, as if they couldn't believe the evidence of their own eyes. Then one of them had slung his rifle and had begun to run off heavily in his thick felt boots. The others had gone to ground and stared at the silent tanks.

'Shit on the shingle!' Schulze cursed to himself and whispered, 'Not a squawk from any of you . . . Anybody who does – I'll shave his balls off with a blunt razorblade.' That terrible threat worked and they cowered in the icy box of the tank, shrouded in silence, waiting for the Ivans' next moves, each man wrapped in a cocoon of his own fears and apprehensions.

Surprisingly enough the Russians had not taken decisive action. Reinforcements arrived in the form of a squadron of Black Cossacks, dressed in their traditional finery, black fur caps tilted to one side of their heads, their dark hair curled in the Cossack fashion. Their *Hetman*, or leader, a giant of a fellow with a sabre slash running down the left side of his dark face, swaggered in the general direction of the two silent tanks, sabre dangling from his waist. He stopped and faced them like David standing up to Goliath. It was as if he were daring whoever was inside the armoured vehicles to open fire on him. Nothing happened. '*Boshe moi*,' he cursed and spat into the frozen snow in disgust. Finally he ripped open his blouse to reveal a naked hairy chest and stood there thus in the ultimate challenge. Again nothing happened. The *Hetman* grinned and shouted something over his shoulder at the waiting horseman. Then he strode forward towards Matz's tank, the only sound the clanking of his long sword.

'*Scheisse*!' Matz cursed. He knew what the Ivan bugger was going to do. He was going to climb upon the turret and try to open the hatch to ascertain whether there was really anyone inside the T-34. With a sinking feeling, Matz knew the time for action had come. Then the wet fart would really hit the wind. He tugged at the leg of the gunner above him in the freezing turret. 'Ten more metres,' he commanded. 'Let him come ten more metres and then give the hairy bastard yer lead.'

'*Zu Befehl, Scharfuhrer*, at your command, Corporal,' the gunner replied in the manner of a green recruit. Matz laughed. The gunner was an old hare like himself. His reply showed that the men were in good heart, trapped as they were, their hooters right deep in the ordure. 'Don't miss then,' he added.

The *Hetman* came on. Once he stopped and, pulling a bottle of vodka out of his pocket, took a deep swig, before replacing the cork and coming on again. 'Cocky bastard,' Matz commented, as above him, he heard the gunner cock his machine gun. Now the Cossack was a matter of seconds before his sudden demise.

'*Ten metres!*' the gunner yelled.

'*Ten metres*,' Matz echoed.

The gunner didn't hesitate. He pressed his trigger. The turret quivered instantly as the machine gun pumped a couple of hundred bullets a minute in the direction of the bold Cossack *Hetman*. At that range the gunner couldn't miss. The Cossack spun round and round, arms waving, as if he were dancing one of his own wild Black Cossack dances. His fur hat slipped foolishly over his right eye, so that he appeared to be drunk, as he slipped to his knees, still waving his arms feebly until he slapped to the frozen snow, dead before he hit it.

The Cossacks had whirled their horses around, making them rear on their legs, flailing their forelegs wildly before they had galloped away to spread the news. The two gunners fired after them. But they weren't very lucky. Skilled riders that they were, the Cossacks ducked to the sides of their mounts using the horses' bodies to protect themselves and, strangely enough, the hardened veterans of front swine somehow didn't have the heart to shoot the animals. Now the Russian attack had commenced in earnest with the first of the 75mm armour-piercing shells of the enemy anti-tank guns screeching flatly through the air, bouncing off the thick glacis plates of the T-34s like glowing incandescent golf balls. Schulze knew it was time to move out. 'Driver, flash your headlights. We're off!' Even as he gave the command, he knew it was going to be a ride through hell.

Four

Von Dodenburg ripped off another burst. The thin line of Russian infantrymen in front of him vanished, as if they had never even existed. Another group came in from the flank. Somewhere behind, 'One-Ball', who had volunteered to come with him, opened up with the MG-34. The Spandau ripped into the Russians, at one thousand bullets a minute. They were galvanized into sudden electric action as that wall of steel hit them. They threw up their arms, danced a kind of macabre jig, as if they were puppets in the hands of a suddenly crazy puppet-master. Next moment they, too, fell to the ground in a gory mess of dead, dying, screaming human beings.

'One Ball', holding the Spandau with his right hand, as if it were a child's toy and holding his one testicle, which had given him his nickname in the regiment, with his left, hobbled on with the rest after von Dodenbury, crying above the vicious snap-and-crack of the small-arms fire, 'Wait for me, comrades . . . wait for me!'

But in his rage and desperation, von Dodenburg was not waiting for anyone. He knew anyway that his handful of volunteers from his First Company would follow him to hell and back. They, too, weren't going to see their comrades and fellow old hares sacrificed to the Ivans like this. For even if Schulze and his patrol were captured alive, they wouldn't live much longer. The Ivans would torture them brutally, as they always did with captured SS men – they even mutilated the corpses of the SS, they hated the 'Black Guards' so greatly – and then they'd slaughter them ruthlessly.

Not that von Dodenburg had any real plan. He felt he had located where Schulze was behind the Russian frontline.

They'd be at the spot from whence the sound of battle was coming. Now all that he could hope to do was to create some kind of diversion with his handful of volunteers in the belief that Schulze would somehow take advantage of it and manage to break through to them.

Now he yelled, '*Los* . . . *Los*,' waving his Schmeisser machine pistol in the direction of the Russians massing in front of him, pulling themselves out of their holes and trenches, frantically pulling on their equipment ready to tackle this handful of impertinent Fritzes who dared to attempt a breakthrough. '*Wollt ihr ewigleben, ihr Hunde?* . . . Do you want to live for ever, you dogs?' He ripped off a blast with his Schmeisser at a Russian about to throw a grenade at him. The grenade dropped from the Russian's suddenly nerveless fingers. It dropped to the ground and exploded in a burst of angry violet flame. The Russian screamed and disappeared for an instant in the burst of flame. When he reappeared, he had been transformed into a dwarf. For a few seconds, while von Dodenburg watched in horror, suddenly transfixed by the terrible sight, he tottered forward on his bloody stumps of legs sawn off at the thighs. Next moment he fell flat on his face and the band of volunteers were rushing on, trampling over his body . . .

'Holy strawsack,' Schulze cried as another anti-tank shell slammed into his T-34. For a moment the interior of the turret glowed an angry dull-red. For a moment Schulze sweated it out. If the solid shot shell penetrated the turret, the razor-sharp steel fragments would whirl around it in a mad lethal fury, killing and maining every human being in their way. Schulze felt the sweat break out all over his body. An instant afterwards the dull glow vanished and the shell went glancing off. They had been saved once again. But Schulze knew their luck would run out sooner or later. The Popovs were tightening their grip on the two tanks as they lumbered forward, crushing and breaking everything that came in their way. It took one cunning shot to the rear of the T-34 or where the turret joined the hull, thus fusing the metal or penetrating it, and they would be done. If they slipped a track, the result would be the same. Next to him in the crowded, icy turret, the gunner chanted the old fatalistic formula, 'For what we are about to receive, let the Lord make us truly grateful.'

'Knock it off—' Schulze began and then stopped short. He could see the reason for the gunner's mock prayer. Outlined in the narrow slit of the turret lookout there was another T-34 heading straight for them, its long overhanging 76mm cannon swinging from side to side like the snout of some predatory monster seeking out its prey. 'Great crap on the Christmas tree,' he exploded, 'look at that steel monster . . . Gunner, traverse right . . . Range two hundred metres . . .' Swiftly he rapped his orders . . . 'On target? . . . *FIRE!*'

In the same instant that the enemy gunner swung his gun round and levelled it on the German tank, Schulze's gunner beat him to it and fired first. Scarlet flame stabbed the gloom. The German T-34 rocked. Instantly the turret filled with the stink of burned explosive. Automatically Schulze turned on the smoke extraction, eye glued to his periscope.

At that range his gunner couldn't miss. The white blur of the armour-piercing shell slammed right into the side of the T-34. It came to an abrupt stop. A track snapped. The gun sank like the head of some monster. Next moment there came a muffled explosion from within the tank and slowly a great smoke ring emerged from the open turret and started to ascend skywards. No one got out.

The first of Commissar Zhdanov's secret T-34s had met its end. But there were still five of the original six left . . .

Von Dodenburg paused and wiped the sweat from his tense, lean face. Now he knew where the missing patrol was and he knew, too, that they were still alive and fighting for their lives. Why else should there be the sound of T-34s doing battle with each other? Russian didn't fire on Russian. Schulze, the incorrigible rogue that he was, had stolen a Russian tank!

He grinned despite the tension of the moment, then he dragged the big bulbous flare pistol from his belt. It was already loaded with the two flares of recognition which distinguished SS Assault Regiment Wotan from all other units of the Armed SS and indeed the *Wehrmacht*. They were silver and black of the elite formation. Raising the pistol above his head, he pressed the first trigger. A soft plop. The flare sailed into the grey sky. It exploded in a burst of bright silver. Immediately the Russians dug in on the attackers' right, started firing at him. But these weren't the expert and feared Russian snipers. These were ordinary Popov infantry, poorly trained in musketry and he knew he could take a chance with his second flare.

He raised the pistol once more, hearing the hiss of the bullets cutting the air all around him, and fired. The flare hushed into the sky to where the others hung suspended, spluttering a bright silver. It, too, burst the next instant, and there blazed the twin symbols of SS Wotan. Von Dodenburg ducked hastily as a burst of machine-gun fire ripped the snow to his front apart and prayed that Schulze would see those symbols.

It wasn't Schulze but Matz, in fact, who spotted that momentary sign of hope as the flares went out, trailing down to earth like fallen angels. But in that instant he was confronted by yet another of Zhdanov's tanks. It came lumbering out of the smoke of the first one, now burning fiercely, followed by a platoon of Soviet infantry crouched low and behind the protection the big tank offered. 'Well, I'll piss in the wind,' he began, caught completely by surprise by the two events. But in the event the little Bavarian corporal reacted more quickly than the crew of the T-34. In the same instant that the Russians brought their gun round to bear on the other tank Matz switched on his lights, turned them off immediately and then turned them once more.

It was an old trick. But it worked. Momentarily the unseen Russian gunner was blinded by the blaze of lights at such close range. The Wotan veterans didn't give him a second chance. The gunner above Matz in the tank's driving seat fired immediately. His first shell howled off the Russian's steep glacis plate, leaving a silver star skewered in the metal, but not stopping the enemy tank. But the old hare manning the gun was still too quick for his Russian opposite number. He fired again. This time he stopped the enemy T-34.

The forty-ton tank reared back on its bogies like a wild horse being put to the saddle for the first time and came to a sudden halt, the turret and its gun fused into immobility. Matz reacted immediately. He drove to the left, his gunner firing wild bursts with his co-axial machine gun to keep the Russians inside their tank rattled. 'Now,' Matz yelled and slammed his head painfully against the gunner's foot above him.

The gunner knew what to do. Now he had the weaker armour of the enemy tank lined up in his sights. He didn't hesitate. Slamming in another armour-piercing round, he fired. At that range he couldn't miss. The white blur of shell rushed towards the unsuspecting Russian. The enemy T-34 didn't stand a chance; there was no hope for it. The shell slammed into its hull. A burst of flame and then the shell had skewered its way through the thinner armour, leaving a smoking silver scar.

Schulze, watching tensely, could imagine what the interior of the T-34 would be like; he had seen such wrecked tanks before. Usually they had to hose out the bloody, gory bits and pieces with a high-power jet of water, piling the gory human remains on the ground like offal at a butcher's backdoor. But one crazed, charred figure, the greedy little blue flames licking up his blackened frame, managed to throw himself from the smoking turret. He staggered a few paces, one skeletal hand stretched out in front like a blind man feeling his way. Next instant, the stricken tank's ammunition locker exploded and the T-34 disintegrated. When the smoke cleared, the man had vanished and the bits and pieces of metal lay everywhere.

Schulze didn't wait to savour his victory. He knew that he had to make the breakthrough now or never. '*Carbide*.' He gave the old Wotan signal for 'speed'. The driver below needed no urging, especially as Schulze had just given him a hefty kick in the right shoulder to emphasize his order. He thrust home one of the tank's dozen or so gears. The T-34's powerful engine roared. The tank lurched forward in the same moment that the Soviet anti-tank guns started firing once again. But their aim was wild and in the turret of Matz's tank which was in the lead, the gunner was spraying a thousand rounds of tracer a minute from left to right, trying to put the enemy gunners off their aim.

Behind, Schulze was trying another old trick to confuse the Russians. At regular intervals he fired one of the smoke dischargers attached to the outside of the T-34's turret. He hoped that the enemy anti-gunners would believe they had hit the T-34 and pause for a moment till the smoke had cleared. By then they would have rolled on and the gunners would have to adjust their sights and range.

Now the two flares designating the position of Wotan were beginning to fall to the ground some five hundred metres away and von Dodenburg, chancing being hit, crawled out of his hole to view the progress of the two steel monsters crawling over the shell-pitted smoking terrain, as armour-piercing shells whizzed back and forth in a white, lethal Morse. Kuno bit his bottom lip with tension. Could they make it? The question flashed through his mind. The two T-34s were out in the open now, with the anti-tank guns ranging in on them from both sides. God, he cursed to himself, how vulnerable they were, and he with his handful of volunteers, virtually pinned down opposite the Popovs, could do little to help them.

Again there was a near miss. An anti-tank shell slammed into the ground just in front of the leading tank and despite the volume of fire, von Dodenburg could hear the shrapnel howling off the T-34's tracks. He clenched his fists and prayed. If a shard of metal snapped one of the steel pins holding the links of the tracks together and the track broke, that would be the end of the lead tank. Some brave fool of a Russian – and there were plenty of them, even among these 'sub-humans', as Reichsführer SS Himmler used to call them – would rush the tank, grenades strapped to his body and die blowing himself and the T-34 up.

But it didn't happen. Again the escapers' luck held out and the T-34, body scarred all over now with shrapnel, kept moving, getting ever closer to the German lines. Von Dodenburg wiped the sweat from his forehead, telling himself that despite the bone-chilling cold, he was sweating like a pig.

But in the lead tank, Matz, also soaked in sweat, knew they were not going to make it in the T-34s; they presented too big a target and every Russian gunner, eager to win himself a bottle of vodka and the Red Star, would now be taking aim at the two escapers, intent on stopping them. The time had come to change tactics and hopefully fool the enemy. It was a trick he hadn't played for a long time: one that back in 1940 had succeeded in fooling the green, buck-toothed Tommies who spent most of their time drinking tea instead of firewater like a true soldier should.

Deliberately he slowed down, as dangerous as that was in itself. Looking up, he yelled at the gunner and his mate. 'In a minute I'm going to stop altogether – for sixty seconds at the most. Come down here and through the hatch. Move like lightning. Got it?'

'Got it, Matzi,' the gunner answered, his face suddenly very pale. He knew just how dangerous Matz's manoeuvre was going to be. One false move once they were through the hatch and the tracks'd churn them up into a bloody mincemeat.

Matz waited no longer. He hit the brakes. The tank stopped with a lurch. In an instant the other two had abandoned their positions and were fumbling and fighting their way over him in the tight confines of the driver's box. The gunner went through the hatch first and lay still on the snow, feeling the hot oil from the engine dripping on to his uniform. His mate followed. He was trembling with fear, and Matz, ready to follow, could feel for him. He was to be next. He drew a deep breath, jammed the controls, and wormed his way out of the escape hatch in the same instant that the T-34 started to crawl forward once more.

For a moment Matz thought he was going to evacuate his bowels with fear. The tracks were churning away only millimetres from his face, the engine heat searing his features frighteningly. Then it was gone with the Soviet gunners ranging in once more, and the three tankers were lying on the ground, their hearts beating like trip hammers. But not for long. Already Schulze's tank was bearing down on them.

Matz pulled himself up, breathing hard through lungs that

sounded like cracked leathern bellows. He waved his arms frantically. Schulze got it. They'd escaped from the doomed tank through the base hatch. He kicked the driver in his box below on the shoulder. 'Halt,' he cried, his voice drowned the next instant by the great hollow sound of steel striking steel. The first T-34 had been hit. It trembled like a live thing and came to an abrupt stop, flames already beginning to lick greedily around its damaged engine.

Schulze didn't hesitate. He knew he'd be next. 'Bale out,' he cried frantically as somewhere in the acrid, choking gloom of gunsmoke, the triumphant Russian anti-tank gunners started to swing their cannon to bring them to bear on Schulze's now stationary tank. There was no time to be lost now, Schulze told himself. With his big paws he fired the smoke dischargers on both side of the T-34's turret. In a flash the tank was surrounded by the thick brown fog. Schulze yelled, 'Jam the gas, driver – and take a powder!' With that he had vaulted over the side of the turret and landed on his feet lightly for such a big man and was running, crouched low, as the T-34 lumbered on in a zig-zag course to disappear in the smoke. They had almost done it . . .'

Twenty-four hours later, the ragged survivors of the suicide patrol and the rest of the Wotan regiment were marched down the same dangerous road that had brought them up the front. This time everything was different. The road had been covered by straw to deaden the stamp of their boots. Despite the inky darkness, Messerschmitt fighters patrolled the night sky to ward off any intruders and again to drown out any sound they might make. At regular intervals mortar crews had been posted on the top of the verges on both sides of the road ready to open fire if there was any Soviet interference. But there was none.

They reached the waiting troop train, steam already raised, to be watched by General Lindemann and the staff, who, huddled in greatcoats lined with fur, watched them as if they were creatures from another world, which, in reality, they were: dirty, emaciated, lice-ridden, but defiant and hating these elegant staff officers, 'the rear-echelon stallions', as the old hares called them. Schulze, a blood-stained bandage around his head where he had been winged by a Soviet slug just as he had reached von Dodenburg, spat contemptuously in the new snow, as Lindemann raised his gloved hand in salute, 'Nice of him, ain't it, Matzi, to crawl out of his gold-plated bunker at this time of the night to see us off.'

'Yer,' a weary Matz agreed, 'you don't see the like of us wild-front swine outside of a zoo these days.' With the last of his strength, he reached up and hauled himself inside the freezing cattle truck that would take them north to Finland and the new front.

Five minutes later they were gone, the red rear lights of the troop train disappearing around the loop in the line. Behind on the platform, General Lindemann shivered and, turning to the waiting heated Mercedes, said, 'Gentlemen, I think we've done our bit for Folk, Führer, Fatherland for this day. I think we deserve a glass of decent champagne, don't you? French champus naturally.' Then they, too, were gone.

BOOK FIVE

The Attack

One

Now von Dodenburg could hear the thunder of the surf on the unseen shore. He knew that the Finns' calcukations were correct. They would hit the tiny estuary that led from the Gulf of Finland to the rear of the German front and from there to Schlusselberg on Lake Lagoda, their objective. If everything went well, they would be able to unload the barges carrying their six precious Tigers: the tank that even the Russian T-34 couldn't stop and the one with which they would achieve their breakthrough, God willing.

In front of him on the deck of the little Finnish patrol boat of the 'Death Squadron', Corporal Matz was being sea-sick, although the water was perfectly calm. Schulze was patting him on the shoulder and saying, 'Poor Bavarian barnshitter, Matzi, you've never been to sea, you and your mountains. All the same, old house, we didn't volunteer to join no frigging navy, did we?'

Matz started to straighten up and open his mouth to reply, but in that same moment he was overcome by another spasm and bent over rapidly to be sick once more.

Despite the tension as the little boat slowed down and those on deck, mostly the women volunteers of the 'Death Squadron', could just make out the faint white line where the surf hit the shore, von Dodenburg smiled to himself. His two old rogues were all right. They'd come through this strange assignment as they had done time and time again. Suddenly he experienced a feeling of confidence. Things would go right, abruptly he was sure of that. He licked the sea salt from his dry lips and prepared for what was to come.

Twenty-four hours before, when they had been briefed by

the little Finnish admiral with the bright blue eyes, von Dodenburg had not been so confident. Admiral Hameenkatu had not tried to paint a rosy picture as he explained the plan alternately in Finnish and German. He shoved his hands on the pockets of his tunic and barked as if he were back on the quarterdeck of the imperial Russian cruiser which he had once commanded: 'Good, let us begin. Now – er – comrades . . .' he hesitated in the form of address as he took in the handful of uniformed women from the 'Death Squadron', 'I won't underplay the dangers. We know the waters around Leningrad. They are unpredictable – the tides, the shallows, currents and the rest of it. With luck, however, our charts will still be accurate. Naturally those coastal waters are bound to be mined and it goes without saying that if we are discovered before we are properly landed, we will be faced by Leningrad's formidable defences.' He had glared at them with those piercing blue eyes of his as if challenging the young male and female officers to say that the mission was not exceedingly dangerous.

No one had dared.

He had continued with: 'However, all is not gloom. We have surprise on our side. General Lindemann's main attack from the south of Leningrad will go in thirty minutes after we have landed and the noise of the Lindemann artillery and the Stuka dive-bombing, once it's light enough to bomb, should give us some cover. But the main thing is –' he turned to address von Dodenburg and Captain Gunnerson, stiff and formal, even masculine, in her blue naval uniform – 'to get the First Company of SS Wotan and their six Tiger tanks ashore safely.' He had clicked his fingers. As if by magic, the door opened and a white-jacketed mess waiter appeared, bearing a silver tray, on which rested tiny glasses of ice-cold aquavit. The admiral took one and waited until everyone had been served, before raising his glass, and snapping something in Finnish, then in German: 'Success to our operation – *Prosit – meine Damen und Herren*!'

As one, they raised their glasses in toast and then when the admiral drank, they tossed the fiery liquid down their throats and threw the glasses into the fireplace, as tradition demanded, where they smashed in a pile of broken glass. It was at that moment, he caught sight of the look in Christiana's eyes. That look of healthy abandon that von Dodenburg had seen there when they had first met had been replaced by one he could only characterize as – despair.

Now the little craft started to feel the tide. The water was being beaten to a white noisy froth and von Dodenburg could only hope that the clumsy barges carrying the sixty-ton Tigers would not capsize. Then, as Sergeant Schulze would have phrased it in his own eloquent manner, 'the tick-tock would really be in the pisspot.' But there was no time to worry about the barges and their precious cargo. Just ahead of them lay the dangerous unknown. For all he knew, the whole of the Red Army lay in waiting for them over there, panting for the dumb Fritzes to walk into the trap.

The tidal race caught them: a fierce tumbling of water over the rocks and sandbanks. Matz was still heaving at the rail, but there was no time to worry about Corporal Matz's seasickness. 'Stand to, Sergeant Schulze,' von Dodenburg cried above the noise. 'Get your people ready.'

On the tiny bridge of the coastal craft, Christiana repeated the same order in Finnish to her little group of 'Death Squadron' volunteers. The girls, for they were all young women barely out of their teens, clicked to attention and von Dodenburg was surprised to see the senior volunteer stepping forward and kissing her Captain's hand, whipping off her sailor's cap as she did so.

Now as they rode the current, von Dodenburg ran his mind over the first stage of the plan. The volunteers and the handful of old hares under Schulze would secure the beach, with the women acting as Finnish interpreters, and, as they all spoke fluent Russian, dealing with any wandering Russians, fishermen, they might encounter. Then they'd signal for the barges to make their run-in with their precious cargo of tanks.

Now as the little motorboat decreased speed, they were caught up in the wild white surge. The craft shook and trembled like live things. Everywhere the Wotan troopers and their Finnish helpers grabbed hastily for stanchions to avoid being thrown off their feet. Matz's vomiting increased even more and an unsympathetic Schulze, holding on to his little running mate with all strength, growled, 'I think I saw your ring coming up, Matzi. Not much more now, and you'll have to crap through yer elbow after this.' Matz's mouth was too full of hot vomit for him to make a reply.

On the little craft went, reeling from side to side, the men and women on deck soaked with the flying spray which ran down their strained, wind-reddened faces in rivulets. Now they were racing through the narrows. Through the flying spray, von Dodenburg, eyes narrowed to slits, caught glimpses of wooden Russian *isbas* – probably the cottages of the fishermen who had once fished the sea in this area. But strain as he may, he couldn't make out a light. He nodded his approval and wished next moment he hadn't as the seawater trickled down the back of his head unpleasantly.

It was when they had almost reached the shore that it happened. Lowering the motorboat's speed to almost stalling, Christiana suddenly lost control of the little craft. It swerved to the right, narrowly missing some rocks which protruded from the white water, only to be swept by the force of the tide to the left. There was a harsh ripping sound. Von Dodenburg was flung off his feet by the impact. Almost immediately the boat started to sink in the shallow water. Men and women plunged into the swirling, freezing water, some shouting, others battling with all their might to keep afloat.

Von Dodenburg went over the side with the rest, thanking God that he had ordered his men to take only their weapons and not the packs. Shallow as the water was, they might well have been dragged under and drowned if they had been burdened by the weight of equipment they normally carried. All the same it was tough. Desperately, he and the rest fought the current, trying to reach the shore before their strength gave out. Here and there men and women didn't make it. They went under with one last cry of despair. But now as von Dodenburg and NCOs like Schulze found they could stand in the surf, but with difficulty, he and they started to drag their comrades to safety till finally they had rescued all who had survived the wreck and they were standing there frozen and shivering, fighting to control their hectic breathing, seemingly alone on this wild, brutal snowbound shore.

Half an hour later von Dodenburg had improvised a primitive signalling system, using driftwood and a tin can of petrol which had floated ashore from the wreck just fifty metres out. Meanwhile Schulze, as always a tower of strength, although most of his men had been too surprised by the wreck to think of their weapons and were thus unarmed, had got them to form a rough and ready perimeter, digging in the best they could in a semicircle around their sector of the beach and waiting for the first sound of the approaching barges bearing the Tigers.

More than once an anxious von Dodenburg glanced at his watch and then cocked his head to the wind in an attempt to pick up the sound of the barge engines. To no avail. All he heard was the howl of the wind and the angry roar of the surf, followed by the slither of the shingle.

Time was running out, Kuno told himself. The barges were already five or so minutes overdue. And if they didn't arrive before Lindemann's main offensive to the south of the beach commenced, all hell would probably be let loose. Once the Russians were alerted to the fact that a major offensive was beginning, they'd make sure that the local defences here would be put on red alert – just in case.

Next to him Christiana cocked her head to the wind and listened intently. He had learned that the Finns seemed closer to nature than the Germans. Perhaps it was due to the fact that they were a rural people, a nation of small farmers and hunters. They seemed to hear and see better that Western Europeans. Now he asked urgently, 'Can you hear anything?'

She didn't answer immediately, but strained even more, while he held his breath, hoping that she'd come up with the news he wanted urgently. Finally she said, 'I think so. Over there to the north. I think they're coming in on the wrong beach . . . behind that cove.'

'Shit!' he cursed. That meant if they wanted to direct the barges on to this beach where they could unload the Tigers with the protection of the First Company's perimeter defences, they'd have to use more signals than von Dodenburg would have liked; and more sigmals would surely attract the attention of the Popovs. He shrugged. He'd have to take that chance. 'Christiana,' he said urgently, 'get your people to light the signal fires.'

She hesitated only a second, as if she, too, realized the danger they'd incur by lighting too many signal fires, then she said, 'Yes, immediately, *Hauptsturmführer*.' Suddenly her arm snaked through his. Tenderly, she whispered, 'Take care, Kuno. We've had enough death.'

Von Dodenburg didn't know whom she meant by 'we', but again there was no mistaking the despair she exuded. 'Of course, dearest,' he replied, making himself sound more confident than he was. 'As we say in German – weeds never die.' He laughed with more confidence than he felt, 'Come on now, let's get those signals lit and those armoured monsters ashore. This war has been going on far too long. Let's show those Monocle Fritzes' – he meant the elegant generals of the Greater German General Staff – 'how to win it – toot sweet.'

Two

Now in a semicircle just above the beach, the lights flickered on, the petrol-fueled fires wavering and threatening to go out in the snow that had now begun to fall. But, von Dodenburg thought, if the snow presented a danger, it also gave them the cover they needed. For already he thought he had heard the sound of motors in the interior. He dismissed that problem, however, as the barges came lumbering in out of the gloom, bearing with them their huge burdens.

Immediately the mixed bunch of soldiers and Finns went into action, wading out as far as they dared in the fast-racing surf to guide the barges in. On the barges themselves, the first of the Tigers was trying to start up, its massive engine making a deep throaty growl. To von Dodenburg it sounded as if the one lone tank was making enough noise to waken half of Leningrad some six or seven kilometres off. But so far there had been no Soviet reaction. Perhaps the Popovs were still sleeping off their daily ration of vodka. He hoped so at least, then in a few moments Lindemann's offensive would commence and then, with the thunder of the air and artillery bombardment, he guessed no one in Leningrad and area would be able to sleep any longer.

'Prepare to land!' someone on the shore yelled and in that same instant the Tiger's massive engine roared into full, ear-splitting noise. There was an instant Russian reaction.

Suddenly, startingly, a finger of icy-white light stabbed the darkness to the left of the beach. The soldiers caught their breath. Von Dodenburg cursed, but still he froze, stopped in his tracks as he hurried to the beach. Slowly the searchlight began to turn in their direction. The light wavered. It was as if its unseen operator had thought he had seen something. 'Holy shit,' von Dodenburg whispered to himself. 'Move on.'

The searchlight did. But in the wrong direction. Instead of moving away from their section of the beach, it proceeded relentlessly in their direction, soon to pin them down in its eye-searing glare. It did, just as the first Tiger, its motor going all out, started to plough its way through the surf towards the beach, to emerge into the full blaze of the enemy's light.

'Holy mackerel!' Schulze moaned, as the light continued to play around the steel monster as if the Russians couldn't believe what they were seeing. 'Shit . . . shit . . . shit.'

Next moment his words were drowned by the crack of Soviet artillery and the sudden burst from the old-fashioned Russian machine guns sounding like the noise of an angry woodpecker. Tracer whizzed angrily through the darkness. Balls of violet flame began to burst on the beach and in a flash all was controlled chaos as the second Tiger struggled though the surf behind the first one, both their machine guns firing wildly to left and right.

Von Dodenburg cursed angrily. The landing was getting off to a bad start. But there was nothing he could do about that. For already to the south there was the first rumble of Lindemann's opening barrage. A scarlet flame lit up the whole sky like the door of some gigantic blast furnace being opened, followed by a roar the like of which von Dodenburg had never heard before in all his years of combat and he knew that Lindemann was employing the whole of his army's artillery, three corps of guns. His confidence returned. In a moment or two the Stukas would be airborne ready for the coming dawn and their murderous bombing of the Soviet installations. They had got off to a bad start admittedly, but surely nothing could stop the massive force the German Army was employing this time to finally break through the Leningrad front and capture the city named after the founder of the evil Soviet Empire. Fresh energy flooding his lean body, von Dodenburg hastened to where Schulze waited with his perimeter defence group. 'All right, you big rogue. Let's get to those Tigers. Take the Finns with you. Let's see if we can earn our pay this day for a change.'

Infected by the CO's enthusiasm, Schulze clapped his massive paws around his mouth and yelled against the ever-increasing roar of gunfire and racing tank engine, 'All right, you frigging heroes, what yer standing there for like a spare penis at a wedding? Get yersens on them tin cans and take the Finnish foreign legion with you – and no feeling them female arses neither. *Dalli-dalli!*'

With surprising energy and enthusiasm after the disastrous start of a landing that had gone wrong, the men and their Finnish women helpers doubled towards the tanks. Von Dodenburg waited momentarily, surveying the scene to the south. Abruptly he was startled by a hand being placed on his arm. He turned. It was Christiana, her face still strained in the ruddy light cast by the artillery bombardment. 'Can I go with you, Kuno?' she asked simply.

He hesitated. He didn't like the fact that he was having to use the other Finnish women of the 'Death Squadron'. But he needed them. Why risk Christiana's life? 'You don't need to go. Perhaps you could be more useful on the beach.'

She shook her blond head. 'I have sent so many of my girls to their deaths. I must take that risk, too. Besides I have no command here –' she lowered her voice – 'and I want to be with you, come what may.'

Von Dodenburg had heard of these northern folk. He guessed it had something to with their long winters when they never saw the sun and spent their time drinking strong alcohol. Still, he hesitated until the last of the Tigers started up and he knew he couldn't wait any longer; soon the Popovs would be bombarding the beach with all they had, and he couldn't afford to lose a single Tiger, if he were going to carry out his mission. 'All right,' he snapped. 'Come on. *Los* . . .' Together, hand in hand, they ran for the nearest Tiger as the first enemy shells started to plummet down on the beach. Watching them run thus, their figures outlined a stark black against the vivid red of the explosions, Schulze growled to Matz, 'Will yer feast yer frigging glassy orbits on that. Don't the CO remember the old Wotan "4-F" motto? *Find 'em, feel 'em, frig 'em and forget 'em.*' Then he shook his big head like a man sorely tried. Moments later they had vanished, heading for the battle to come . . .

The Russian attack came suddenly, surprisingly, although they knew that sooner or later the Russians would counterattack. At dawn von Dodenburg had ordered a stop. During the night he had taken terrible risks driving his tanks forward in the darkness, where a simple Russian private armed with an American bazooka could have knocked out a Tiger, unprotected as they were by infantry.

Now as they paused at a rundown abandoned Russian village and attempted to brew coffee and make pea soup, while the rest of the Wotan came up to offer the armoured spearhead infantry protection, the first Russian infantry came sneaking out of the snow-heavy fir woods to their right like predatory timber wolves. As usual the Russians wore camouflaged overalls in white and came out of the trees in twos and threes noiselessly; indeed some of them moved forward to the attack on skis.

Then when they were within a hundred metres of the village, they dropped any pretence at silence and crying that frightening bass '*Urrah*!' of theirs, they rushed the village on both flanks. Almost immediately a wild firefight broke out as the men and women who'd been trying to light fires in the open broke down the doors of the nearest cottages, frantically hammering at the unpainted wood with the butts of their rifles, desperate for cover. But already they were taking casualties. Schulze, who was heating a can of 'Old Man' on the exhaust of his Tiger, saw one of the Finnish women go down, her blouse ripped apart to reveal her plump breasts riddled by what looked like a series of red buttonholes. '*Himmel, Arsch und Zwirn!*' he yelled in rage. Ignoring the hotness of the can of meat, reputedly made from dead old men at Berlin's workhouses, he hurled it at the Russian. The can hit him in the face and he went down shrieking. Next moment an equally angry Matz thrust home one of the gears and before the Russian could get up, the sixty-ton monster had rolled over him, squashing him to a bloody pulp under its broad tracks.

Together with Christiana, von Dodenburg rushed for the protection of another Tiger. A group of Russian infantrymen tried to stop them. The Finnish girl fired from the hip and one of the Russians was lifted clean off his feet and was propelled backwards, as if struck by a giant fist. Von Dodenburg was quick off the mark, too. He had no time to fire his weapon, especially at close quarters. Instead he slammed the metal butt of his Schmeisser into the unshaven face of the nearest Russian. He reeled back, his noze squashed to pulp, thick gobs of blood pouring from it and staining the snow at his feet.

Von Dodenburg felt the hot blood spurt across his face. It didn't worry him. Carried away by fear and fury, he smashed his weapon into the Russian's face once more. He heard the bone snap like a twig underfoot in a wood on a hot day. The Russian dropped and then they were through and the two of them were running all out for the nearest Tiger . . .

Now Schulze took over the defence, while von Dodenburg tried to raise the Vulture and report what was happening, for he suspected the Russians had reacted quicker than Lindemann had anticipated and were counter-attacking all along the front. Schulze was in his element. Yelling obscenities at the Russians – '*Frigging garden dwarves*' . . . '*Popov piss pansies*' . . . '*Arses with ears*' – he and his fellow tank commanders kept the Russians at bay with short, sharp bursts of their turret machine guns in between moving the position of their tanks every few moments; for Schulze, the old hare, knew it would be disastrous to stay in the same spot for long; it would have been an ideal way of being blasted to hell by some Russian stalker armed with a bazooka.

'No time for putting things into code,' von Dodenburg snapped at the radio operator who was bleeding from a wound in his hand. 'I'll take over and report in clear.'

'Sir,' the operator replied. He was a greenbeak and obviously scared as bullets whined off the Tiger's turret. But he was barely eighteen and von Dodenburg knew he was doing his best as he tuned and whirled the dials, trying to raise the Vulture. But there was static and calls everywhere; the air was thick with them and von Dodenburg guessed he was right.

Not only had Lindemann launched his offensive, but the Russians had reacted swiftly with what was perhaps a major counter-offensive. He bit his bottom lip as the operator, hued a pale green in the light of the turret, twisted and fine-tuned, obviously wanting to please his CO. Then he had it. He passed the earphones over swiftly and, wiping the operator's blood off them, von Dodenburg relayed his urgent message immediately. 'Sir, at the moment we're bogged down at . . .' He gave the map reference, not giving a damn that the Russians would be listening in to his message as well. 'We need panzer grenadier support immediately. Can't risk my tanks without infantry, sir. Over.'

The Vulture's voice was distorted by the static, but there was no mistaking the harsh rasp of a Prussian officer. 'What do you mean, you can't risk? We are all taking risks. As soon as I can, I shall dispatch infantry support to you. Now you must push ahead—'

'But—'

The Vulture didn't give him time to object.

'Move out now. Get me one tank on the shore of Lake Lagoda and I'll recommend you for any piece of tin your heart desires. Over and out!' The radio phone went dead, leaving von Dodenburg to stare at it, as if in blank incomprehension.

Three

By midday of that day the great German surprise attack on the Leningrad Front was slowly halting. The Finns were still attacking and moving south from their own country towards Lake Lagoda. But their army was too small and lacking in armour to make the decisive breakthrough and cut the only source of supply for the besieged garrison of Leningrad, that across the Lake. Only the Germans could do that. But the German drive was weakening by the hour. Now it had become a bloody slogging match between the attackers and the Russian defenders in well-prepared positions, aided by their customary winter ally, General Frost. For the weather had become terrible: snow, hail and temperatures so low that men left out in the open too long were found frozen stiff, dead at their posts.

Later the generals would explain to the Führer that their plan must have been betrayed to the 'Reds' by spies. It was a convenient fiction that Hitler would accept, for he believed that there were spies everywhere, even in the High Command, and this saved the generals from dismissal or even worse.

But on that day, the generals were explaining nothing to Hitler; they hadn't the time to do so. They were too busy trying to save what could be saved. As ever, more alarming reports came flooding into their headquarters, with the telephones ringing constantly, demanding more troops, more artillery, more planes. They and their staff officers, shocked and white-faced, did the best they could to keep the front from breaking. They pleaded, cajoled, lied, promised, threatened – anything they could think of until General Lindemann at his HQ decided what should be done next. While they did so their soldiers died by the score, the hundred and later by the thousand: cannon fodder dying for 'Folk, Fatherland and Führer', but in fact for no useful purpose.

Lindemann, as always, played his usual big, bluff hearty role of a senior officer who had seen it all before and could not be shaken by bad news from the front. He also procrastinated, while all around him his staff lost their heads, telephones jingled incessantly and mud-splattered dispatch riders roared and skidded into the courtyard below, bringing ever-fresh tidings of woe. For in truth he didn't know what to do. If he continue to attack, he might well lose too many men, perhaps even his army. If he failed to attack, he risked Hitler's wrath. He had not spent half a lifetime working his guts out on a miserable salary in order to reach his present rank and then to lose the rank and the pension which would be his after the war was over because he failed to take the right decision. At his age he knew he wouldn't get a second chance. But what was the damned right decision?

In the end, surprisingly enough, it was that pervert and lowly colonel in the SS, Obersturmbannführer Geier of SS Assault Regiment Wotan, who helped to make that decision for him. Normally as army commander he wouldn't accept calls from officers below the rank of full colonel, but Geier was in the SS and a favourite of Reichsführer SS Himmler and, as things were now, he judged it wise to keep well in with Himmler. So he accepted the call, wondering as he did so what tale of gloom and doom Geier would relate.

So he was surprised when Geier, his voice sounding confident, snapped, '*Herr Generaloberst*, I wish to report that I have six Tigers safely landed and undamaged, which I have just ordered to make a dash for the shore of Lagoda as planned. There to link up with the Finns until the Colonel-General's forces reach the spot. I await your further orders, *sir*.'

Lindemann could have burst into tears. It was the way out. He was already sure that Wotan didn't have a chance. There was probably no match for the Tiger on the Russian side, but when – *if* – the Wotan tankers reached their objective and took up a defensive position, they didn't stand a chance against the mass of the Russian infantry with their American bazookas and the like. So it would be Hitler's darling SS which would have seemed to have failed, not his own men of the *Wehrmacht*. God was looking down on him favourably after all, this terrible day.

Voice full of fake confidence, he replied, 'I'm relying on you, *Obersturmbannführer*. The whole operation may sink or swim on the basis of what those six Tigers of yours can achieve. Believe you me, Geier, there's promotion in this for you.'

At the other end the Vulture gave one of his crooked smiles. 'Naturally, sir, I cannot give you a one hundred per cent guarantee that the mass of my regiment will be able to reach the Tigers on any kind of schedule. But you can rest assured that we will do our utmost. The honour of the Armed SS is at stake, sir.'

'Well said, Geier!' General Lindemann boomed, happy now that Geier also didn't seem so confident about making a success of the mission. 'It's good to have subordinates like you under my command who don't lose their heads when things appear to look black. Whatever happens – and you have my word on it – you will receive your well-earned reward. Good luck. *Ende*.' He put down the phone, and rang the bell on the big desk in front of him. His orderly appeared at once, almost as if he had been waiting at the other side of the door. Lindemann clapped his fat beringed hands. 'Come on, Horst. You know it's time for my champagne breakfast. Bring on the bubbly. I won't warn you about being late again. It'll be back to the infantry if you are.'

The harassed orderly fled and General Lindemann sat back in his chair quite pleased with himself . . .

Ten kilometres or so away, the Vulture was pleased himself, too. He seemed to have covered all angles. Naturally he would make an attempt to reach that arrogant young swine von Dodenburg and his Tigers on the shores of Lake Lagoda, if he ever got that far. But he certainly wasn't going to throw away his whole regiment doing so. Whatever happened – and he had feeling that it was going to end in a fiasco – he wanted to have a command when it was all over. Now he had Lindemann's backing – and the fat pig was running scared, that was obvious – who would be in a position to criticize him? He laughed suddenly. Von Dodenburg might, he supposed, but by then he would be dead . . .

It seemed to von Dodenburg that their luck had changed. The sudden snowstorm had caught both sides by surprise. In a matter of minutes visibility was down to ten metres. The Russian attackers appeared to vanish and abruptly the six Tigers were ploughing ahead in a column on their broad tracks designed for the Russian winter alone, the noise of their engines muted by the snow coming down in dense steady sheets. Huddled beneath a tarpaulin on the hull of Schulze's tank, protected a little by the ten-ton turret of the Tiger, von Dodenburg felt the Finnish girl press closer to him, as if she wanted to soak up as much of his body warmth as possible. He patted her absently and tried in his mind's eye to remember the details of the trail they were to take to the Lake.

It had been worked out to take them clear of any villages of hamlets where they might meet resistance. For in winter in Russia, neither side, Russian nor German, would attempt to spend more than a couple of hours outside in the country's freezing temperatures. Indeed, that winter, most of the fighting at an infantryman's level had been, not to gain tactical advantage, but to find a place of shelter for the night.

The fact that they were avoiding the villages meant, von Dodenburg told himself, the only enemy they might have to contend with would be Russian armour, or perhaps marauding Cossack cavalry. But at the steady fifteen kilometres an hour they were travelling over the featureless plain, even the enemy's mobile forces would have difficulty finding them.

So, he concluded, with a bit more luck he might make it now. Then it would depend how quickly the Vulture could move the regiment without any motorized transport, save for a few reindeer sledges supplied by the Finns, to join him. In the meantime he'd form a perimeter defence with his Tigers, backs to the Lake, using whatever infantry he could find among the Finns, including the women, to make up a kind of loose perimeter. It wouldn't be an ideal solution, but he was assuming that the Russians wouldn't discover his presence immediately in this terrible weather and every hour saved until the battle commenced would put the regiment another kilometre closer to him.

He pulled down his hood and put his mouth closer to Christiana's ear. 'Your girls,' he shouted, 'are they all armed? I might need them. Everyone who can fire a rifle would be useful.'

She nodded and yelled back, 'We are the Death Squadron, aren't we? Kuno, we are all dedicated to death. We won't survive the war.' Now the despair in her voice was mingled with fatalism. 'We don't expect to.'

'Silly.' He tried to brush it off. 'Why should your girls die, or anyone of us for that matter? It is the business of a good soldier to survive and make the enemy soldier die.'

She muttered something which he didn't catch and for a while they lapsed into silence, listening to the roar of the engine, as they ploughed through that snowbound waste. Huddled there under the canvas, they might well have been the last people alive in the world. Von Dodenburg told himself, he really ought to push back the canvas and peer outside, but it was just too cold to do so. Besides he could tell from the green-glowing dial of the compass strapped to his wrist that they were keeping the course he had plotted for the armour to Lake Lagoda. So he huddled closer to the girl, letting his mind wander, remembering how he had cursed the sweltering heat of Iraq the previous year and how he wished he could enjoy some of that sane heat now.*

It was about then that he felt her hand wander down to his loins. She had taken off the thick felt-and-fur glove that the Finns wore and he could feel her searching fingers quite plainly. As cold and preoccupied as he was, he became excited immediately. His mind flashed back to that scene at the sauna when she had offered him her buttocks to beat in atonement

* See L. Kessler's *Operation Iraq* (Severn House) for further details.

for God knew what and how the sexual cruelty had thrilled him in a manner that he had never been thrilled before. For a moment he was tempted to tell her to stop. This was a military operation. Men's – and women's – lives depended upon him. But then she had found her way through his thick clothing into his flies and he forgot his duties; he was too excited. Gently she stroked his member into tumescence. He grabbed her excitedly. But she pushed him away, whispering, 'It has to be this way, Kuno. Don't worry. I wish to give you pleasure.' There was a sudden sob in her voice; he didn't know why. But she was exciting him so wildly that he no longer cared. She moved her fingers up and down ever more quickly. He started to gasp, as if he were running a long race. Nothing mattered now, just the culmination of that race. Up and down. Ever firmer. He sobbed for breath, mouth wide and gaping and ugly. Thus they loved in their fashion: a kind of loving that was as coarse and brutal as the life they lived at the front. It was a love that could only end in death.

Some two hundred metres behind the last tank, the Cossacks had dismounted, ignoring the snow coming down in solid sheets, their mounts already white with it. The guide, half Cossack, half Mongol, from one of Russia's remote Asiatic provinces, bent and rubbed away the new powder snow to reveal the hard-pressed rectangular block beneath and then another one. He turned and grinned up at the sergeant holding the lantern to illuminate the area. 'Tank,' he said in his oddly accented Russian. 'German tank.' He grinned even more as the sergeant nodded his approval. 'You give me vodka now?'

The Russians had found the Tigers.

Four

'Did I ever tell yer about the pavement-pounder I picked up in Munich back in '39?' Matz cried through the intercom as the tank continued to plough steadily through the raging snowstorm.

'Ner,' Schulze perched in the turret next to the gunner, both of them freezing in the ice-box of a tank, dewdrops hanging from their red noses, growled, 'but yer gonna tell me.'

'Thought it might warm yer up,' Matz replied.

'Go on, get on with it, Matzi. Piss or get off the pot.'

'Well, once we'd decided on the price of a mattress polka together, I sez to her, being the perfect gentleman, I allus am, "What about showing me yet tits first?" I'm like that, you know, all heart.'

Schulze gave a mock groan. 'Get to the frigging sex part, willya?'

'All right, all right, I'm getting to it. So she unloosened her two bras and—'

'*Two* bras?' Schulze cried.

'Yer, didn't I mention it already? Yer see, Schulzi, she had two pairs o' tits.'

'You mean two – *four tits*, real 'uns.'

'Yer, proper milk factories. She could have looked after four nippers easy with tits like that. Well, as I was saying, knowing how cunning them pavement-pounders are, I asked her if there would be any hidden charges for the tits, especially as she had two pairs of 'em.'

'And?'

'And she sez, only if I wanted a jelly roll or anything like that. Now, I ask yer, Schulzi, how can a squaddie ask for a jelly roll in daylight in the middle of the English Garden?' He meant the celebrated Munich Park.

'Get yer.' Schulze licked his cracked, swollen lips at the thought of two pairs of plump breasts. 'What happened then?'

'I had an idea.'

'Get on with it. The way you're rabbiting on, it'd take yer all yer time to have a stiff one.'

'Well, I said to her, if I paid her a bit extra would she let me—'

Schulze, agog now for whatever Matz had posed to the whore all those years before, gave one last glance through the turret slit before devoting all his attention to his running mate in the driver's compartment down below. What he saw drove all thoughts of sex out of his mind. A brief glimpse through a break in the snowfall made him grab for the turret machine gun with one hand and press the throat mike with the other to cry in alarm, 'There's frigging riders out there – Cossacks!'

Next moment, to the rear, where Tiger Six brought up the rearguard, there was a sudden burst of angry red flame and what had to be a Molotov cocktail, an improvised fire grenade made up of a vodka bottle filled with petrol, exploded on the Tiger's deck. Next moment the snow closed in again, blotting out the fire-stricken rearguard tank. But Schulze had seen enough. The Popovs had tumbled to them. Blindly he fired an angry burst into the falling snow as the lone Cossack disappeared as swiftly as he had appeared.

The two greenbeaks and the Finnish woman, faces terrified and blackened by the smoke of the burning tank, fell to their knees, hands high in the air, crying in their abject fear. '*Nicht schiessen, Kamerad . . . Tovarisch, Paschalsea . . .*' Almost immediately, the Finnish girl, who knew better than the two Germans what was going to happen, started to sob bitterly.

Despite the falling snow, the Cossacks took their time. They gawped at the size of the burning tank, not even worried as the locker ammunition started to explode, sending tracer bullet whizzing in crazy zigzag into the sky. '*Bolsho . . . Boshe my* . . . How big.' Then as the Tiger began to detonate, they backed off slightly, indicating with their whips and sabres that their three prisoners should do the same.

Still on their knees in the snow, crying bitterly, arms held bolt upright, the three of them did as ordered. The *Hetman*, still on his fine black horse, which had turned white in the snow, jerked his knout in the direction of the Finnish girl. He meant her to get up. She did so, still weeping, her whole plump body trembling with fear.

The *Hetman* looked her over. He twirled his fine black moustache like some villian in an old-fashioned melodrama. Suddenly, and with surprising energy for a middle-aged man which he was, he vaulted cleanly over the head of his mount, dropped catlike in front of the woman and in that same instant ripped down her trousers still smouldering from the tank fire.

The watching Cossacks guffawed. They knew the *Hetman* was regarded as a great lover. Now, despite the weather and the danger of their present position, he was obviously going to demonstrate his prowess for them.

'*Davoi*,' the *Hetmann* commanded the nearest Cossacks. Two of them stepped forward. One, a giant with a pock-marked face, grabbed the girl and raised her aloft, getting a good feel of her breasts as he did so. The other knew exactly what to do. He ripped the screaming girl's knickers from her nubile teenage body with one fierce tug.

'On her knees,' the *Hetman* ordered.

'*Da*,' the pock-marked Cossack obeyed. He grabbed the girl again and forced her head between his booted knees so that her white rump stuck in the air. The *Hetman* smiled lecherously and twirled his black moustache once more. The next instant he ripped open his black breeches to reveal his erect penis sticking out in front of him like a policeman's truncheon.

The watching Cossacks gasped as if in awe. For a moment the *Hetman* posed thus so that his men could enjoy the sight. The next, he nuzzled the screaming girl's rear with the tip of his erection. Desperately she bucked and twisted, but the pock-marked Cossack held her between his knees easily, enjoying every moment of her screams of fear and the display which was to come. 'Let's hope she's a virgin, comrades,' he yelled exuberantly, 'then we'll see some blood.'

The delighted Cossacks yelled and clapped and whistled between their fingers in the Cossack fashion, as the *Hetman* grunted and pushed. It was the last thing he ever did. The chatter of the Schmeisser machine pistol at close range caught the. Cossacks completely by surprise. The *Hetman* was hit first. His rakishly tilted fur hat slipped ludicrously from his black curls and he sank to the snow, dying as he did so, still clutching his penis, as all around him his men died too and their mounts, seized by a sudden panic, galloped away into the white-out, leaving their masters to die moaning where they lay, the snow pelting down to cover them already.

Von Dodenburg and Christiana dropped down from the hull together, as Schulze whirled the turret round, already on the lookout for any new enemies.

For visibility was still down to less than ten metres and it would be easy for another Cossack patrol to sneak in almost noiselessly and deal with his Tiger as they had done with the one that the greenbeak had driven.

The girl had fainted and, half naked as she was, von Dodenburg knew she could easily die on them in these sub-zero temperatures. He lifted her, while the Finnish girl stripped the dead *Hetman* of his fine black coat and draped it over her. Together they carried her to the deck of the Tiger and placed her body on the exhaust cowling from which the heat of the engine escaped. Then von Dodenburg turned his attention to the smouldering Tiger, while Christiana stroked the unconscious girl's hand lovingly, muttering to her in Finnish.

The interior of the ruined Tiger was the usual bloody mess of a knocked-out tank. A charred body hung by the throat mike – it was the radio operator – in the turret. Down below in the driver's compartment, the body of the driver still bubbled with the intense heat generated by the exploding Molotov cocktail. Red patches oozed liquid to the blackened skin, where the surface of the body had burst and exploded in the heat. He turned away hastily, the hot vomit flooding his throat. He had seen tanks like this destroyed in the battlefield often enough in the last years. But he had never grown accustomed to the sight; it was too horrible.

He dropped back into the snow, which had now almost covered the two dead greenbeaks and the Cossacks. Over in Tiger One, Schulze called, 'Better not wait much longer. In this snow we'll easily lose the column, sir.' Schulze hesitated and then added, 'What's the drill now, sir? The Popovs have twigged us . . . There'll be more of them, sir, and we don't have the infantry protection we need in this kind of weather . . .' His voice dropped away, as he saw the sudden worried look on his CO's face.

It was the same thought that had just been going through von Dodenburg's mind at that moment. The ease with which the Russian Cossacks, using the earliest form of mobile warfare known to man, had dealt with the latest, the supposedly impregnable Tiger, worried him. Without infantry protection, another Cossack patrol, armed with primtive Molotov cocktails – petrol, a bottle, a bit of rag and a match – could knock out his tank next. The rest could follow. Now the Russians were alerted and under the cover of this terrible snowstorm could approach the Tigers with impunity; what chance did they stand of reaching the shores of Lake Lagoda?

Slowly, thoughtfully, von Dodenburg walked back to the Tiger, its engine ticking away solidly like a metal heartbeat. The assaulted Finnish girl had lapsed into unconsciousness. Christiana turned to face him, her eyes tender, but full of hurt. 'Why go on?' she asked without preliminaries. 'They know we're here. How many times will this happen?' She stopped short and indicated the girl beneath the dead *Hetman*'s coat.

'Duty,' he answered dully and, reaching up, clambered on to the hull of the Tiger.

'It's always duty, Kuno. There must be an end to it. We must think of ourselves, as individuals.' There was a note of pleading in her voice now.

'I – all of us of the SS – have sworn a sacred oath of loyalty to the death to our Führer. We cannot go back on that oath when things get tough or our own lives are endangered.' He drew the tarpaulin over her frozen body, but remained outside it himself this time, Schmeisser at the ready. He knew it wouldn't be long before they had to face up to other attacks.

'Then you must die,' she answered coldly. She turned and, closing her eyes, pulled the tarpaulin over her head.

'Yes – death,' he repeated, but she wasn't listening. He shrugged and shouted to Schulze in the turret, 'All right, you big rogue – carbide!'

This time Schulze didn't respond as he would do normally to the SS slang for 'give her gas'. Instead, he kicked Matz's shoulder in the driving compartment below and pressing his throat mike, scowled, 'All right, piss-pansy, move off.'

Matz didn't respond to the supposed insult. He was in no mood to do so. Instead he selected one of the Tiger's many gears and rammed it home. The great Maybach engine roared and they were away once more, spraying the dead bodies lying in the snow next to the burnt-out Tiger with a white wake. Seconds later they had disappeared into the raging storm and left the corpses to be buried in this remote place for all time, unless the wolves found them first.

But as they rolled towards their objective, every man – and woman – tense and apprehensive, wrapped up in their own thoughts, gloomy as they were, von Dodenburg knew they were doomed if the Vulture didn't turn up with his infantry in time.

The Vulture, however, was taking his time. He advanced at a snail's pace, knowing that General Lindemann would now not put any pressure on him to speed up his progress. Instead he set the speed of his 800-strong regiment in line with that of his reindeer-drawn sledges and the reports of his Finnish patrols who ranged far and wide to each flank to ensure that Wotan didn't bump into any Russian ambush.

Occasionally the regiment encountered wandering patrols of Soviet cavalry, which so far Wotan had been able to drive off by musketry but which the Vulture had made no attempt to follow up and eradicate so that they didn't report the presence of the Fritzes advancing on Lake Lagoda. Why should he? If the Russians used the information acquired by the patrols and made a massive attempt to stop Wotan's further advance, that would be that. It would be the excuse the Vulture would use if there was ever an inquiry into his conduct at this time. Despite the terrible weather and the increasing number of Russian patrols his Finns were encountering on their reconnaissance missions, the Vulture was in a good mood. At any time now, he could order his force to withdraw – so far the Wotan regiment had suffered only a handful of casualties – and return to base relatively intact. As the little voice at the back of his mind said every now and again, 'Don't worry, old house, those general stars Lindemann almost promised you will be yours soon.' But the little voice lied and Obersturmbannführer Geier would live to regret his shameful failure to support von Dodenburg and his Tigers.

Five

The shore of Lake Lagoda was roughly one kilometre away now. Visibility had improved greatly. Just before dawn the snowfall had ceased and as dawn broke with a blood-red ball of sun appearing on the horizon, the fresh snow sparkled and glittering in its cold rays. On any other occasion, the scene would have looked beautiful, something that could have been used as an illustration for a pre-war Christmas card in the homeland. But not now. As von Dodenburg blinked at the scene, red-eyed and weary, telling himself it would only be a matter of days before it really was Christmas 1942, he knew beautiful weather like this could only bring trouble for the little armoured force.

Indeed as the five Tigers drew up under the cover of a wood of firs and the weary Germans and Finns started to make their traditional pea soup breakfast, melting down the green bricks that made the soup, the trouble that Kuno had predicted would come, came. It did so in the form of a strange *tack-tack* noise to the south. It puzzled the greenbeaks, but not the old hares. Immediately they shaded their eyes against the glare of the rising sun and searched the icy-blue sky until they found what they sought. 'Sewing machines,' a couple of them attempted to enlighten the puzzled recruits.

'Sewing machines?' the others echoed.

Schulze laughed scornfully and drained the last of his carefully hoarded flatman. 'Don't you kids know nothing? When will you get off'n yer mothers' tit? It's a Rata, a Popov spotter plane. You can't mistake the noise a sewing machine makes . . . sounds just like some old granny working on her sewing machine.'

Von Dodenburg had recognized the old familiar warning noise, too. But he wasn't happy with the recognition. Once the Rata had located them, he'd be off to report to his base. Before long the Soviet dive-bombers, the Stormoviks, would be zooming in, ready for the kill; and his little group had nothing in the way of anti-aircraft weapons save their handguns. 'Get into those trees,' he ordered sharply. 'You, Matz, take a bead on the sewing machine if you think he's spotted us.'

Matz, the Bavarian farmer's son, who had the keenest eyesight of all Wotan's old hares, nodded his understanding.

'Drivers into the trees too. Cover the tank tracks as soon as you've done so. They'd be a dead giveaway.'

The men needed no urging. Immediately they set about their tasks. The drivers felt their way into the firs, trying to avoid snapping them off and revealing their hiding places to any aerial observer, while Christiana and her fellow Finns panted hard as they pushed fresh snow over the broad tracks left by the Tigers. Slowly the now ominous noise of the Russian spotter plane came closer and closer, as it zig-zagged back and forth across the pilot's map co-ordinates, making it clear that the Russian had been alerted to their presence and was definitely looking for them. Von Dodenburg cursed. As he had turned and run for cover he had caught a fleeting glimpse of the sun sparkling off the ice to his left. He knew instinctively that had to be the iced-over Lake Lagoda. It meant they were in striking distance of their objective, and now this was happening. Christ on a crutch, it was damn unfair. Then he laughed at himself and whispered, 'Now when has war ever been fair, Kuno von Dodenburg?'

'What did you say, Kuno?' Christiana gasped as she threw herself into the powder snow next to him. Her face was flushed a bright red with the exertion of covering up the tank tracks and her blue eyes sparkled with health.

'Nothing,' he began, 'just something silly—'

He stopped short. Matz had broken the tense silence of the men and women hiding in the firs with, 'There she is . . . south-south west . . . And she's coming in very low.'

'Down – get your faces down,' von Dodenburg snapped

urgently, as the little spotter plane rose over the snow-heavy firs, its prop wash shaking the snow from them it was so low. Indeed von Dodenburg, watching the slow little biplane swerving in curves above the forest, thought the Rata had already lined them up roughly; the pilot knew where they were. Now he was trying to plot their position for the follow-up aerial attack. He bit his bottom lip. Even the Tiger's thick hull armour wouldn't be proof against the Stormovik's bombs. What should he do? Try to knock the damned 'sewing machine' out of the sky before it could report back to its base? Or should he take a chance that the Rata in the end wouldn't be able to spot their exact position?

But the decision was taken from him. With startling suddenness, the result probably of a warm and cold front meeting over the lake, von Dodenburg reasoned later, a thin mist appeared. It swept in from the water, curled about the trees like some grey cat and immediately obscured them from the air. The relief was almost palpable. He felt Christiana's body relax to his. The tension was broken immediately. Here and there men grinned at each other as if they had achieved something. Others in the turrets of the tanks relinquished their hold on their machine guns.

Sergeant Schulze didn't share the relief of the others. He growled to Matz as they ate the steaming hot pea soup, their dirty, unshaven faces wreathed in the steam, 'Don't trust the Popovs as far as I can throw their arseholes.'

Matz raised his nose, which was virtually inside the canteen of soup, and was dripping with green beads, and asked, 'Why don't yer, Schulzi? . . . Trust 'em.'

''Cos that Popov pilot was a cunning shitehawk. He'd spotted us all right. He knew if he'd have come lower we could have shot him out of the frigging sky, the speed he was going at, so he took advantage of the mist to do a bunk.' He finished off the last of his soup with a flourish and before he started to lick out the bottom of the canteen, added sombrely, 'We ain't heard the last o' that plane. Take my words for it, Matzi.'

Half an hour later, the mist having lifted as abruptly as it had appeared, the little column was on its way again, its crews' spirits uplifted by the hot soup and the ease with which they had escaped the threat posed by the 'sewing machine'. Things were going well. They were going to make it after all.

By mid-afternoon that December day, they had reached the shore of Lake Lagoda, the ice sheet which covered it and made it the Russians' sole means of supplying the besieged city of Leningrad glistening in the cold winter sun. While von Dodenburg took a little patrol with Schulze, Christiana and a couple of riflemen to check the area, the rest dug in their Tigers the best they could, though the permafrost made it virtually impossible to dig very far. So they were forced to do their best with branches stripped from the nearest firs to camouflage the metal monsters.

Over to the north, the watchers from Wotan could just make out another column of Russians crossing the ice very slowly and in extended order (to avoid breaking the ice under their weight), heading for the beleagured city. Further on, where the ice hadn't formed, small fishing boats and barges were bringing up the heavier supplies. But as far as von Dodenburg could ascertain, neither of the two groups had noticed their presence, so far. He told himself that if he were in the Russians' position, he'd be in too much of a hurry to get to the safety of the other side and *terra firma* to worry about what was going on on the flanks.

He handed the glasses to Schulze and let him survey the position for a few minutes before asking, 'What do you think, Schulze, you big rogue?'

Schulze licked his frost-bitten, cracked lips before saying, 'Easy as falling off a log to nobble that lot. Think of all the Russian grub for the taking – and the vodka.' He licked his lips again.

'Think about the tactical position instead, Schulze,' von Dodenburg chided him gently.

'First off, sir. No good for our Tigers. Sixty tons on that ice. No sir. We'd go through the ice like shit through a goose.' He turned to Christiana. 'Please forgive my French, Captain. We rough-and-ready soldiers—'

'Knock it off,' von Dodenburg interrupted him hurriedly.

'We want none of your sweet talk. We all know what a damned rogue you are.'

The Finnish woman laughed. 'Soldiers are always the same,' she said, as if that explained everything. 'But with your Tigers you have a power base. I have been told by my comrades that those 88mm cannon of yours have a tremendous range. They'd be able to cover any attack on those convoys over there.'

'You mean infantry attacks?' von Dodenburg asked swiftly.

'Yes.'

Next to them, Schulze growled, 'But where's the shitting stubblehoppers, sir? So far there's no sign of the rest of Wotan.'

'I know . . . I know,' von Dodenburg answered testily. It had been the same question that had been plaguing him ever since they had arrived at the shore of the lake. They had done what was expected of them. But without the infantry to support an attack at the base of the lake, cutting it off as a supply route for Leningrad, what purpose would they serve here? Besides, sooner or later, they would be discovered by the enemy – they had been lucky that the 'sewing machine' hadn't discovered them earlier on – and then all their effort would have been for nothing.

Von Dodenburg made up his mind. He rose carefully, saying, 'I'm going to contact HQ.' Crouching low – just in case – he doubled back to the lead tank, where Matz was showing one of the plump young Finnish girls the Tiger, his hands firmly clenched around her delightfully plump bottom as he 'helped' her to mount on the hull.

Von Dodenburg grinned and then snapped, as if he were the typical company commander of the Armed SS, 'Corporal Matz, put that woman down – this instant.'

Matz took his hands off the girl's buttocks in a flash and the girl flushed a deep red. Von Dodenburg winked and said, 'All right, Matz, you'll be able to show our Finnish comrade the way in half a mo. I need the radio.'

Matz understood. 'Yessir, I'll show her – *the way*.' He winked too.

Moments later von Dodenburg, earphones pressed tightly to his cropped blond head, was searching the airwaves, trying to pick up Wotan. As on the day before, the air waves were full of static and garbled messages which indicated, von Dodenburg felt, that Lindemann had resumed his offensive to the south. But where in three devils' name was the Vulture and the rest of Wotan?

Then he had the regiment's call sign. Hurriedly, he adjusted the set.

The Vulture himself came to the radio phone. He listened to what von Dodenburg had to say about their present position, the two of them using a private code this time in order not to give away von Dodenburg's exact position to the enemy radio detection troops.

The Vulture congratulated Kuno grudgingly and then the latter posed the overwhelming question. 'We have been buzzed by Soviet reconnaissance planes, sir. However I don't think they have located us exactly. But it won't be long before they do. What is the drill now, sir? *Over.*'

The Vulture didn't hesitate. 'It is vital that you maintain and hold your present position, *Hauptsturmbannführer*. I am doing my utmost to reach you, and as you may have already heard, our friends from the south are pushing forward, too.' He meant General Lindemann's army. '*Over.*'

'*But when*, sir?' von Dodenburg asked almost desperately, not trying to hide the concern in his voice. Under present circumstances, once the Popovs had located his tanks, which they surely would soon, his little force probably wouldn't last the day.

'I am doing my best under very difficult circumstances,' the Vulture replied, pleased that he was making the arrogant young bastard squirm at last; von Dodenburg was losing that celebrated iron control of himself, it seemed. 'You can accept that I will try my damnest, von Dodenburg. *Over and out.*'

The radio phone went dead and abruptly von Dodenburg realized with clarity of a vision that the Vulture would never attempt to link up with his little force. He was on his own. He had to make his own decisions. Should he retreat now or hold on till he couldn't hold on any longer? Either way he would be caught by the short and the curlies; and if he survived the debacle he would be court-martialled for dereliction of duty. In the German Army in 1942, to retreat without orders meant a virtual death sentence. He clambered out of the turret, his head whirling and in turmoil with conflicting ideas.

That was not the case at Govorov's headquarters. The intercepted radio message and the report put in by the Rata pilot moved through channels at a surprising speed for the bureaucratic Red Army. Reduced to half a page of staff paperwork, there it was. The Fritzes had reached Lake Lagoda with a small force of these formidable new tanks of theirs. They were without infantry protection – that was clear from the various radio messages and the nearest, this SS regiment, was not making any desperate attempt to reach their tanks.

Govorov didn't need a crystal ball to know what he should do. He turned to his waiting chief-of-staff, and snapped, 'Throw the Red Guards regiment in the path of these Fritz SS men. I want them stopped dead.'

'Yes, Comrade General.' The clever-looking chief-of-staff scribbled a note hastily on his pad. 'And the tanks?'

Govorov shrugged carelessly. 'Do the obvious. Don't waste men on them. Let the flyboys take care of them. My order is – *liquidate them*!' He snapped the pencil he was holding in his right hand with the force of his words. 'Liquidate *every last one of the Fritzes . . .*'

Six

Von Dodenburg avoided thinking the inevitable. Instead he made his dispositions, which he hoped would cover both eventualities: hold on to the position on the Lake or retreat. He guessed he was on his own now; the decisions were up to him. And of one thing he was sure. Regardless of the consequences to himself, he was going to ensure that his men and their Finnish assistants had a fair chance of surviving.

So he and his command toiled, preparing their primitive defences with what material they had – and there was precious little save for the Tigers, and they might, in the end, be a hindrance rather than an asset. To both flanks they laid out a primitive anti-personnel minefield. It consisted of what the men called realistically but cruelly 'deballockers'. These were prepared so that when any unwary soldier stood on one of them, it flew into the air at waist height and did what its name implied: emasculated the unfortunate soldier.

To the front, facing the lake, he positioned two Tigers in a hull-down position to tackle any enemy soldiers who attempted to attack from the ice, plus two small infantry mortars to break up the ice with their bombs if the Russians did attack. To his rear in the forest, he placed his remaining three Tigers with a covering force of dug-in riflemen. This, von Dodenburg knew, was his most controversial disposition. In any court martial he would be severely criticized for placing the bulk of his little force in a position from which they could retreat. Von Dodenburg didn't care at that moment. He was going to save his men if he could. Besides, they gained confidence from the move. It meant their CO was not going to sacrifice them worthlessly; he was going to allow them a chance to get away.

That afternoon, as the little force went to ground, just in case the new Russian convoys sent out patrols to their flanks to check the nearest shore, where they were dug in, the 'sewing machine' came over again and this time they knew they had been spotted. It wasn't that the Rata circled directly above them. Instead it kept its presence just out of range of the Tiger's machine guns, and the old hares realized immediately what the pilot and his observer were up to. They were trying to get the outline of the Tigers in the slanting rays of the December sun which were penetrating the close-together firs. In this way they could count them and decide what kind of resistance they could expect from the Fritzes.

'*Scheisse*!' Schulze cursed impotently as he followed the course of the little plane with his machine gun. 'Now the tick-tock really is in the pisspot!'

It was, but not only for von Dodenburg's little command. Some ten kilometres away, the Vulture's column was advancing at a snail's pace over the white waste of the plain that led to the Lake. The Vulture was taking no chances. He had flank guards out and a thin line of skirmishers to his front. They stopped whenever there appeared to be approaching a spot where danger might lurk; they were acting on the Vulture's express orders. For the hook-nosed officer had decided that at the first sign of trouble he would pull back and use the trouble as an excuse to retreat to his startline. Indeed at that moment, as he focused his glasses to his front yet once again, he would have welcomed trouble and the chance to get out of this goddam barren killing ground.

But when the trouble came, it came from a totally different direction from the one he had anticipated. Like silent silverfish the Stormovik bombers glided in from the rear. In the very same instant that the startled lookouts turned in the direction of the intruders sliding almost noiselessly through the hard blue wash of the winter sky, the Russian pilots opened up their engines to full throttle. Above them the barrel-like Yak fighters zipped through the bomber formation and came screaming in at tree-top heights, weaving crazily from left to right, machine guns blazing, spitting bursts of angry purple fire at the totally surprised Wotan column.

Men went down everywhere. Reindeers were hit too. Wild with pain the half-wild animals threw their loads, overturned their sledges, scattering men and supplies everywhere on the snowfield. In a flash everything was chaos and confusion with men firing wildly at the little fighter planes which blotted out the sky, they were coming in so low; while others, some flinging away their weapons in their panic, ran frantically for cover.

Moments later the Stormovik dive-bombers fell out of the sky. They came down at an impossible angle, in what appeared to be a dive of death from which the pilots would never be able to pull the planes. Then, in the very last moment when it seemed that the planes must smash into the ground and disintegrate, the pilots threatening to blackout with the g-force at any second, they pulled back the stick and levelled out. A myriad lethal black eggs fell from their silver bellies and then the planes were soaring high into the air once more, while down below the bombs exploded in bursts of angry violet flame.

The Vulture, as cruel and cynical as he was, was no coward. Standing in the midst of the chaos with metal flying everywhere in great red-hot shards, he raised his pistol and fired at the attackers, crying above the roar of engines and the crump of exploding bombs, 'Take cover . . . for God's sake – *take cover*!'

Frantically, his men ran to obey his orders, abandoning the sledges and the dying reindeer, struggling on their forelegs to rise, their sides flecked a bright scarlet with blood. But while they did so, the Vulture realized, as he stood there amid the bloody chaos, that he had suffered enough casualties to stop his relief operation. As angry and shaken as he was, he knew that SS Assault Regiment Wotan's part in the great attack on Leningrad was over. He could retreat and save what was left of Wotan with a clear conscience. He had done his duty. If, at that moment, he wondered what fate would befall von Dodenburg and his Tigers some ten kilometres away, he never made any reference to it later.

Minutes later the combined force of Yak fighters and Stormovik bombers struck von Dodenburg's force dug in in the forest. This time their target was more difficult to find, especially as the mist was starting to creep in from the lake once more. But still the dare-devil pilots of the Yaks tried. Once more they came in at tree-top heights, their prop wash lashing the firs into a green frenzy, deluging the snow into flurries upon the men cowering below.

This time the Yak pilots tried a new tactic. Coming in from both flanks, missing each other by metres as they flashed by one another, they fired red tracer into the trees in the hope of setting them alight and burning away the Tigers' cover. But they had miscalculated. The firs were too damp from the snow to have the resin in them set alight. Instead the trees began to smoulder, adding to the density of the mist creeping in from the lake.

Still they tried, while below the men and women cowered and waited for the inevitable; for most of them thought they didn't stand a chance with the tubby little Russian fighters almost on top of them, dashing back and forth, pumping tracer into trees which pattered down on the tanks like heavy tropical rain on a tin roof. It was then as the raid reached its crescendo, that one of the Tigers' drivers panicked. Later it was discovered he was one of those callow greenbeaks who had joined Wotan in Berlin in what now seemed another age.

Suddenly, before anyone could stop him, he fired the engine. Flame sprang from the Tiger's exhausts. With a groan and lurch, the big tank rose out of its hole. Branches used to camouflage the steel monster fell to left and right as it moved forward. Snapping off firs like matchwood, it burst out of the forest into the open. It was a fatal move. The frustrated Yak pilots, realizing that ground visibility had almost gone and they would have to break off their attack at any moment, fell on the lone tank with all their fury.

Zooming in below the mist, they came roaring across the snowfield, spitting cannonfire in a vicious hail. The panicked tank driver didn't have a chance. As the others in the wood watched, aghast, the driver attempted to zig-zag and dodge the cannonfire, the best he could.

But he hadn't a chance. Shells ploughed up angry spurts of flame in the snow, hurrying towards the sixty-ton tank. The first burst caught the Tiger in the turret. Great silver scars appeared at once as if they were symptoms of some terrible skin disease. Another Yak took over. The pilot came in from the flank where the Tiger's armour was thinner. This time the shells punched right into the tank. All sixty tons of it reeled visibily. Von Dodenburg groaned and cried, though he knew the greenbeak driver wouldn't be able to hear him, 'Bale out . . . bale out while you've got time!'

But the greenbeak felt he could still get away, although by now tiny puffs of grey smoke were escaping from the Tiger's hull, indicating that something inside it was on fire. Now the greenbeak no longer attempted to zig-zag to avoid the cannon-fire. He drove the tank straight ahead. It was a fatal move. As Schulze moaned, 'By the great whore of Buxtehude where the dogs piss through their ribs, what are you doing, you idiot? You're play—'

He never finished his protest. In that very same instant, the third Yak took aim on the fleeing tank coming up from the rear, its weakest point. Cannonshells peppered the slow-moving Tiger. Angry flames shot up high. A track came off and abruptly the great steel monster was stranded in the middle of the snowfield, its severed track reeling out behind it like an amputated limb. Next instant it went up completely, the great 88mm shells exploding in its shell locker.

Von Dodenburg turned away as the blast hit him in the face like a blow from a flabby fist. When he turned his head back again, the Tiger had disintegrated, transformed into a mess of grotesquely twisted metal. On the trees opposite, their bark stripped by the force of the explosion, gory-red bits and pieces of flesh hung like some horrible human fruit, dripping a dark juice which was blood.

Christiana gripped von Dodenburg's arm. 'It is enough,' she said thickly and then, turning away, still holding on him, she started to vomit violently.

Von Dodenburg knew it was enough. Once the mist cleared, the Russian planes would be back, he was sure of that. But could he abandon his position here, the leading element of the leading German unit, the spearhead of the whole Lindemann army, because his fate seemed sealed? His great-grandfather had charged with the Prussian Guard at Mars-le-Tour in the Franco-Prussian War when he had known he would inevitably die doing so. His grandfather had been massacred by the natives in German South-West Africa because he had tried to tackle a mob of rebellious Hereros single-handed. It had always been this with the von Dodenburgs. Even when they had known they were going to die, they had not run. They had done their duty and died. Was he not bound by that same centuries-old tradition?

Two hours later when the mist had cleared once more and in the evening gloom they could just make out the plumes of black smoke rising into the evening sky to their rear, von Dodenburg knew that there was no reason for him to hold the position here on the bank of Lake Lagoda any more. The offensive had failed. 'Schulze,' he called quietly to where Schulze was trying to brew up the last of their peppermint tea on a little fire.

'Sir?'

In a voice that displayed no emotion, only an infinite weariness, he said, 'We've had it, Schulze. Get the men ready. We pull out within the hour.'

Schulze touched his hand to the rim of his helmet. He said nothing. He knew any comment would be superfluous. Instead he walked back to the rest and kicked some earth over the blue-flickering fire of twigs and said, 'All right, comrades, pack yer stuff . . . We're going home to mother.'

Nobody cheered.

Envoi

'Well, Kuno, you have returned to the slaughterhouse, I see . . . with most of your parts still intact.' Professor Major Martens of La Charité gave the son of his old friend General von Dodenburg a tired smile.

'Good morning sir,' Kuno answered, a little wearily, too. 'Again I can't give you my right hand.' He indicated with a jerk of his head his right hand and arm, which were fixed in a splint covered with plaster of Paris that came level with his right shoulder.

'Ah, they've given you a "Stuka", I see,' Martens said almost cheerfully. 'That should keep you out of mischief for a while.'*

Von Dodenburg didn't comment; his mind was still full of those last hours of the column before the one single remaining tank had reached Wotan's lines and he had been able to sink into the blessed oblivion of unconsciousness at last. That ten-kilometre stretch between the lake and where the Wotan had dug in after the bombing attack, ready to retreat once they were in position to do so, had been a nightmare. They had been attacked by the fast-riding merciless Cossacks time and time again. They'd swoop in out of nowhere, roaring their fierce cries, using their horses as cover, firing from beneath the saddle, oblivious to their losses, knocking out tank after tank, sweeping the terrified fugitives from their decks as some giant might use his great hand to sweep away importuning flies.

In the end there had remained one tank, Schulze's and

* Named after the gull-winged Stuka dive-bomber. *Transl.*

Matz's, with the two old hares using all the tricks they had learned in three years of war to keep going and fend off the Cossacks. But even they could not help the men and women crowded on the hull behind the turret much. Time and time again, Schulze sounded a warning for the fugitives to duck and then he'd spray the Cossacks riding up to attack them from the rear with vicious bursts of fire from the turret machine gun. The attackers went down by the dozen, their cruelly injured horses dragging their dead masters with them, covering the snowfield with their scarlet blood.

It had been just half a kilometre from the Wotan line when the final disaster had happened. It had been a break in the constant action and those on the hull had been reloading their weapons when the Cossacks had attacked again, coming this time from a totally different direction that they had anticipated.

Abruptly, fire was pouring into them from the rear. Von Dodenburg, who had taken over the command of the men and women packed on the Tiger's deck had reacted immediately. But the survivors, most of them out of ammunition, had not met the new threat so swiftly. Matz, the old hare, down at the tank's control, realized that from the volume of fire. To protect those above, he had wrenched the Tiger round to meet the new attack. With fatal results. One of the Finnish women and two of the greenbeaks had been caught off guard and fell to the snow.

Immediately the black-clad Cossacks had urged their mounts forward, yelling their war cries, eager for the slaughter. It was then that Christiana had gone a little; in retrospect Kuno could not think of a better description. In the same instant that the first of the Cossacks, a bearded giant with a pock-marked face, had raised his gleaming sabre to slaughter the Finnish woman, Christiana had dropped from the hull, firing from the hip as she dropped.

The Cossack had been swept from his mount by the volume of her fire at such close range. But it hadn't helped. Another had come galloping in, the foam bubbling at the muzzle of his mount, its coat gleaming with sweat. He yelled something and, raising his sabre, had brought it down with all his strength. The girl's unprotected skull had been cleaved neatly in two red halves like some ripe autumn apple. Christiana had screamed and raised her machine pistol. But she never had a chance to use it. The Cossack sergeant had come bursting from the trees, showering himself with snow, lance already levelled. It had caught her straight between the shoulders. Her back had arched like a taut bowstring. The blood had begun to pour from her gaping mouth at once. She had dropped to her knees, gasping and choking on her own blood, the lance, snatched from the sergeant's hand by the force of impact, still quivering violently in her back. Next moment as the grenade exploded which would nearly severe Kuno's right arm, she dropped face forward, dead before she hit the ground.

Now the professor said, as Kuno prepared with the rest of the badly wounded for his session with the masseur, 'You're damn lucky, Kuno – or are you, I wonder? You nearly lost that arm. That would have put an end to your fighting career.'

For a moment Kuno von Dodenburg didn't respond. Instead he looked around at the other young officers, most of whom were in a worse state than himself: limb stumps purple and red, gutted by frostbite and shell splinters, crippled for life when they were hardly out of their teens. 'Duty,' he said, the first word that came into his head at that moment.

'*Duty*,' the professor sneered. 'What does that mean? Will these poor devils try to explain their wasted lives, years of being cripples, looked at by other people as some kind of abomination, with that one word? I doubt it, Kuno.'

'Sir –' Kuno von Dodenburg forgot his own problems. The way his father's old friend and comrade was talking was dangerous; one couldn't trust anyone these days. 'You must not talk like that in public. Please.'

Martens shrugged and gave up. 'But what a waste. Perhaps you're right. By the way, there are two of your men here to see you. Very rum pair indeed, but they insist on paying their respects, as they put it, but I have never seen in all my professional career two less respectful persons than that couple.' And with that he was gone, leaving Kuno to watch in horrid fascination the young Panzer lieutenant with no legs, who had removed his trousers, complete with artificial limbs, and was now hopping on his stumps to where the masseur was waiting for him.

Stiffly Kuno von Dodenburg walked down the stairs, stinking of Lysol and human misery, trying to avoid looking at the two officers with two and a half legs between them, clutching each other's shoulders like lovers, helping themselves up the stairs. 'Couple of your fellows downstairs,' the taller of the two said, 'kicking up a tremendous racket. *Schwester* Klara's going totally *meschugge* with them.'

Kuno groaned. It would be typical of Matz and Schulze. They were probably drunk and up to their old tricks. But as slow as he was, by the time he reached the two of them Sister Klara had disappeared, though there was mysterious noise coming from the cabinet in the adjoining room. He ignored it, for as Matz and Schulze clicked to attention, faces highly flushed, which indicated they had been drinking, his gaze fell upon the young woman who seemed to be with them.

She was a bleached blonde, her breasts bulging from her low-cut blouse and, despite the coldness of the February day, she wore a skirt so short that it made Kuno feel if she bent down, she'd be arrested for gross indecency. 'Sussi,' Schulze announced grandly, spreading his paw in her direction like a head waiter ushering a favoured customer to the best table in his restaurant. 'She gives a good time to gentlemen like yourself, sir, who can't use their hands when it comes to a clinch on the couch.' He winked knowingly and Sussi, eyes sparkling, licked her little pink tongue around her lips.

For a moment Kuno was puzzled and then he understood as Matz added, 'She's a present from us and the old hares of the First Company. Even the mean shite Zieman, who counts his money under his bunk in the middle of the night, chipped in and that says it all.' He beamed at the pale-faced young officer, his arm raised in the 'Stuka'.

'Well, it's kind of you and the others,' Kuno stuttered, taken aback a little by the nature of his 'present', who was pouting, her scarlet-slashed lips wet and trembling violently, as if she couldn't get down to the business of 'giving a good time' to officers who 'couldn't use their hands' soon enough. 'But this is a hospital. You can't do that sort of a thing in a hospital, not in La Charité at least.'

Schulze winked again knowingly. 'Don't you worry yer head about that, sir. We've worked it all out with – er – Sister Klara. Why she's offered you her own quarters for the job.' He grinned. 'I believe, sir, she'd even give you medical assistance if you found it difficult to do – hm, you know what I mean, sir.' Next to Schulze, Sussi was gyrating her hips wildly now, her skirt riding up to reveal she wasn't a true blonde.

Kuno's mouth dropped open. 'In three devils' name, Schulze, you'll get yourself court-martialled for this. Now get that woman—' The rest of Kuno's words were drowned abruptly by the blare of the military brass band, playing '*Preussens Gloria*', and the harsh stamp of hundreds of steel-shod boots.

Their eyes shot as one to the large hospital window which let on to the main street below. Abruptly it was packed with people: Hitler Youth stalwarts waving paper swastikas, the girls of the Hitler Maidens bobbing up and down in their short brown skirts excitedly, a few severe-looking women from the *Frauenschaften* throwing weary bunches of flowers – and the recruits.

Eyes fixed on some distant horizon known only to themselves, heads raised proudly, faces flushed with youth and determination, they marched rigidly behind the garrison band, the name of their new regiment proudly emblazoned on their sleeves – *SS Assault Regiment Wotan*.

'*Himmelherrje*,' Matz exclaimed in his thick Bavarian accent and, surprisingly enough, crossed himself. 'The greenbeaks – the new boys.'

'More cannonfodder – for the chop,' Schulze growled and stopped short when he saw the look on the CO's pale face. He realized that the zest had gone out of the day. The CO wouldn't need the whore who looked after 'gentlemen who couldn't use their hands', not this day nor many to come. He guessed von Dodenburg's mind was back at the Front, that great burial mound of metal and human flesh and the ghosts, as wan and grey as their uniform, who inhabited it.

Soon they would be going back there, together with those young hopefuls down there, urged on by the bellows that the 'Bull' made on such occasions. Schulze shook his head. Slowly the sound of the boots, the bands, the cheering, died away and the three of them looked at each other in sombre silence, the whore forgotten now.

It seemed a long time until von Dodenburg broke the silence, his voice remote and strange. 'It can't happen again – *to them*, can it?' It wasn't a statement. It wasn't a question. It was a plea.

But neither of the two old hares had an answer to the CO's plea. They remained stubbornly silent, frozen there, as if for all time . . .